MEMOIR
DELAWARE COUNTY PRISON

REGINALD L. HALL

Writersandpoets.com, LLC

Published by Writersandpoets.com, LLC

Cover design by www.mariondesigns.com

ISBN 0-9703803-3-X

Library of Congress Catalog Card Number 2003115587

Author's note: The names have been changed and characters and situations have been altered to protect the identities of those involved.

First Printing: January 2004

Second Printing: March 2004

Printed in the United States of America

Writersandpoets.com, LLC

Post Office Box 1307

Mountainside, New Jersey 07092

sales@writersandpoets.com

This book is dedicated to my mother, Theresa B. Hall. Besides my Lord above, you are my only sunshine. You are my shelter when it storms, my strength when I feel weak, my wisdom when I am confused, and my eyes when I cannot see clearly. You were there for me when no one else was. Thank you.

I Love You Mom!

-Delaware County Prison-

Introduction

You know, when I was young, I used to watch old movies where the bad guys always ended up going to jail; when I got older I watched my brothers go to jail. I never believed that same thing would happen in my life, not until the day I found myself walking through those metal doors. I've been witness to things I never knew existed, and I did things I never thought I'd do. The eight months I spent in jail were the worst months of my life. Being in a place where I'm told what to do, when to do it, and how to do it was not right for me. Although I knew it couldn't rain forever, that the sun had to shine at some point, at times it seemed the sun would never shine my way again.

Delaware County Prison (D.C.P.) is a place I never want to see again. I now understand I scared a lot of family members when I started talking all that shit about suicide, but I just wanted out of there. No one knew what it was like, taking showers in nasty tunnels, going to the bathroom in front of numerous people. Never have I been so embarrassed or humiliated in all my life. And I cried. Lord, how I cried. Even through the laughter, and there was laughter at times, my heart still wept. Getting back home was my focus, and at times it seemed I would never make it. It was more than just a home-cooked meal that I needed; it was the peace that comes from being with those I truly love.

I was about at my limit when I had to sleep on nasty metal beds and eat off of dirty trays. But there was nothing I could do. I made my bed and I knew I had to lie in it. Being confined behind brick walls, away from the people I loved, was lonely and scary. I vow, I will never see that place again…being gay in the military is one thing, but being gay in jail is a whole different thing. I'm glad to be home.

Intake

As I walked through the steel doors I cringed as I heard them close tightly behind me. I looked at the other inmates' faces, wondering how I got here. This place is not for me. I hated to be locked up, caged in anything, let alone jail. Ahhh, things I should have thought about beforehand. Walking up the steps was scary; I knew in my gut that this was just the beginning of a very tough time. The strip room was next, an unbearable thought, and yet my feet stumbled that way.

"Take off all your clothes," barked the correction officer (CO). I really didn't get a good look at his face—maybe I didn't want to, more likely I was ashamed. I took off every strip of clothing, down to my underwear.

"Remove those too," he stated clearly. Humiliated, I bent and removed my underwear. As I stood, I looked into his face and saw no expression whatsoever. I wanted to scream about the injustice that was being done, but this was my fault. I had no one to blame. As I stood there naked, I thought about all the things I was going to miss. I had no idea how long I'd be there. All I knew was that the judge stated that if I could get my detainer lifted, I could go home. Lord, how I wanted that to happen. Standing there I realized that it wasn't so much that I felt scared, it was more the waiting and being around so many different people that was beginning to wear on me. Early on I had a feeling that I wasn't going to get home for some time, so I should just try and relax. I felt the cool air coming from the air conditioner. It felt good. I stood there and tried easing my mind from all the stress that had been building up in me for some time. I had known for a long time this day was coming, I just didn't know when. It would be good to get it over with. Just as I was coming to grips, the CO ordered, "Now turn around, bend over and spread your butt cheeks."

"Now turn around and lift up your testicles and spread back your penis."

There was nothing I could say. I felt so violated. When he finished the exam, he tossed me a brown shirt and a pair of brown pants, along with a plastic bag, which contained a bar of soap, a comb, a plastic spoon, a plastic cup, a small tube of toothpaste, a toothbrush, and a small bottle of some cheap deodorant. I could feel tears coming, but I was determined not to cry.

I was led to a small holding cell that had three benches and three telephones. There were about ten others in there, niggas, all waiting for the nurse. I couldn't believe this shit. I couldn't believe that I was even a part of this. The phones were free but there was no one to call. My mother was at work, so I waited. How long am I going to be in here? This question kept repeating itself in my mind. I turned and asked one of the COs how long I'd be in this particular cell.

"Just until you see the nurse," he replied.

I started feeling at ease when other people started cracking jokes on each other. The jokes were about two cute guys in the bunch, Shawn and Rahim. They seemed about my age, eighteen, or at least Shawn was. Rahim was about twenty-five. I couldn't resist, first I looked at his face, then I glanced down at his dick print, but there was no dick print in sight, not in these brown shapeless sacks. I talked to the other inmates for a bit but gave up. No one was talking about anything, just how they came to jail, what happened the last time they were here, how long they stayed, and on and on. Here I was, wearing a brown suit that did not match my black Timberland boots, no dick print to speak of, just sitting there, thinking about my pretty smile—which was not smiling. At least six hours later the nurse finally arrived. By that time it was about one o'clock in the morning. Everyone in there was so tired. The nurse began calling names in alphabetical order. Knowing I had a good while before she would get to the letter H, I called my mother.

"Hello," she said in one of her many soft voices. I could tell I woke her up.

"Mom, I'm in jail," I said quietly.

"In jail for what?" she asked.

I explained the story to her as best I could, just giving the basics such as the credit card scams combined with me already being on probation. I also explained I probably wouldn't get out anytime soon because of the detainer, even if she paid the $750 bail. She told me she'd try to get the bail money but she couldn't guarantee it. I hung up. Again I had the strange sensation that this was all a dream. I wished it were this time yesterday, or even better, this time last year.

"Reginald Hall?" the nurse called out my name. I got up and walked to the gate where the nurse was. I had to stand there until the CO came and unlocked it. As he walked toward the gate I could hear his many keys jangling by his side.

"Are you Reginald Hall?" he asked.

"Yes," I replied.

He unlocked the gate and I walked across the hall to the nurse. I had never felt so hopeless in all my life. When I got into the little room I saw that she was a small lady. She seemed harmless. But still I was scared. I sat down next to her metal desk where I saw a box that looked like it contained a lot of needles. As she asked what my middle name was she walked me over to the scale where she took my height and weight. My brown-skin body was ten pounds overweight. She sat me down again and started asking a lot of questions. Had I ever done any drugs? When was the last time I had sex? Did I have a history of illness? I was so distracted by the box of needles, it took me a minute to follow her questioning. Before I knew it, she had a needle out of the pack and was tying a thick rubber band around my arm.

"I'm just going to take some blood," she said. I looked down at the size of the needle and jumped back before she even stuck me. I hate needles. When she finally found a vein and inserted the needle, I screamed. I could see the inmates across the hall laughing.

"You big baby," she said as she placed a cotton ball and tape on the hole.

Intake was so dirty—chewing gum stuck in the steps, old trash bags littering the hallways, cockroaches scuttling by. I would soon find out that the roaches weren't just in the intake area.

By two a.m. I was hungry as hell. I was sure they weren't about to give me that cheesesteak I'd been craving all week.

"Time to go upstairs," the CO called. Fuck, I was tired.

We all walked upstairs in a single file line. I tried to keep my distance from the crackheads and thieves, but it was no use, we were all headed to the same cell. When we got there, I quickly climbed onto a top bunk that was closest to the wall. Taking my sheet from the CO, I rested my head on my arms and instantly fell asleep. I slept good. I could've been at home cuddled in my bed under my warm comforter, with clean sheets and big soft pillows. I was jarred awake with the call for "chow up." A yellow shirt runner for the jail had brought around five trays with pancakes and sausage. I jumped down off of my bed and began eating— despite the fact that I could see the remnants of old spaghetti on the trays. What the hell, I was hungry. After I finished eating I got back into bed and slept for another couple hours.

"Okay, let's go," the CO yelled. It was time to see the counselor. We all went back downstairs. I started cracking jokes with Shawn and Rahim, trying to make myself feel more at ease. We waited in the holding cell for a couple of hours before they brought lunch around: hot dogs and baked beans on the same dirty-ass trays. I knew this was gonna be hell. I hadn't eaten hot dogs for over ten years, and didn't feel the need to start. I just left the food sitting there. It wasn't long before some old guy scarfed it down.

"Okay, time to go upstairs," the CO called.

"I thought we was supposed to see the counselor," I said.

"You can see her tomorrow," he responded, indifferently.

Back upstairs we went, to the same cell. My cellmates started talking, passing the afternoon. I was bored as hell. I glanced over at the other cells where more people were coming in off of the street. They looked terrible, like they hadn't bathed in weeks. I paced around the cell. In the corner was a sink, attached to a toilet. I had to take a shit bad but I wasn't about to go to the bathroom in front of all of these people.

As the loud gates closed throughout the prison I started to get a creepy feeling. This place was bad. I jumped back up on top of the bunk bed. I couldn't concentrate because of all the trash talking that was going on below—it was like we were at some kind of social event or something. I lay up there, not being able to sleep with all the noise, the clanging bars, the sound of keys, and the relentless chatter. When I finally did fall asleep I forgot where I was. Again, I slept like a baby. I slept through dinner, waking in the middle of the night when someone got up to take a piss. I could hear the stream hitting the floor, completely missing the toilet.

Now I really started to get the creeps. Walking barefoot in the dark, I heard the man going back to his bunk, stepping in his own piss as he climbed back into bed—unconcerned about washing his hands or flushing the toilet. I didn't even want to dwell on it.

The next day I heard the CO walking around for awhile before stopping at our cell. "Let's go see the counselor." Here we go again, I thought. I jumped down from off the top bunk and practically ran out of the cell—anything for a change of scenery. Back in the holding cell we went. I sat in the corner hoping no one would say anything to me, or even brush against me. I was dirty. I was sure I smelled; even my underarms were itching. So were my feet. I glanced around the dirty cell; looked up at the ceiling and then down at my hands. I prayed that God would have mercy on my soul. I was about the seventh person in line waiting to see the counselor. I just got up and started pacing the twelve by twenty-four-foot cell.

The counselor called my name, "Hall. Reginald Hall,"

I walked across the hallway into the same cell that the nurse was in the night before. The counselor looked at me and smiled. I smiled back. I sat down in the same chair. My heart was beating at a slow pace. I felt calm, but mostly I just wanted to go home. I looked down at the bandage that was on my arm from where the nurse had poked me with the needle. I kept glancing outside of the room looking at the other inmates.

Finally, I asked the counselor when I was going to get out of here. She smiled again and told me she didn't know the answer. Well at least she told the truth I thought. She stood up and turned on the air conditioner.

"That feels much better now," I told her. She smiled again. I started a conversation, asking her different things, like how her day was and where she bought her outfit. I was being very pleasant. I was hoping she'd tell me I was a nice kid and she was gonna arrange things to get me back home. But it didn't work out that way. Instead she started asking me a lot of questions that I was not in the mood to answer, but I answered them anyway. Finally she asked me what block I wanted. I told her E-block and then asked if I had a detainer. She told me no.

"My bail is $750, and without a detainer I can get out on bail?" I asked.

"Yes, you can post your bail and get out because there is no detainer," she said, still smiling.

I screamed, "Yes!" That was when we were about done. As I was getting up to leave, she looked around on the desk and removed a couple of papers, uncovering a small piece of paper that read *D-E-T-A-I-N-E-R*. I looked at her and she looked at me with that same silly-ass grin on her face that I could've just smacked off. But I really wasn't too surprised.

"Sorry, I didn't see it," she said. I walked back across the hall.

Going to see her was useless, no help at all. I waited in the cell with the rest of the dirty people, waiting until it was time for us to go upstairs. When it finally came time, I climbed up the dirty metal steps with the rest of the group. This time I knew I had to use the toilet. My stomach was starting to hurt and I couldn't hold it. My first time taking a shit in D.C.P. I went into the cell, took one of my bed sheets, and tied one end to the gate and the other end to the bedpost, creating a semi-private shitting corner. As soon as I sat down, about three heads popped up. Now ain't that a bitch? It didn't make any damn sense. Clearly there were a few freaks in here.

E-block

When they called my name to move me to E-block, I was lounging on the top bunk—feeling quite a bit better.

"You're going to E-block," the CO said. I quickly gathered up my sheets as he opened the gate. I walked by him slowly, and then walked down the steps, but I had to wait in a line because I wasn't the only one being processed to a block. As I made my way toward E-block I realized I was starting to smell exactly like the jail. Processing included posing for a mug shot and receiving an inmate number on an armband, number 981571. That was me from that day forward.

As I waited to be moved to E-14, I looked around at the day room where we were standing in line. There were three stone tables, similar to what you might see in a park, and seven telephones, collect calls only. As I glanced down the line I saw the first guy that I thought was kind of cute. His name was Ronald, Ron for short. He was actually more than cute. He was downright handsome. He stood there in a white t-shirt, a pair of blue gym shorts he bought from the commissary, bright ankle socks, and a pair of slippers. He was a nice chocolatey tone, curly hair, broad shoulders, and most impressive, his nice, juicy, pussy-suckin' lips. He turned and looked at me, then looked down at my wristwatch.

"How much you selling that watch for?" he asked.

"It's not for sale," I responded.

"Well how much did it cost?" he asked. I just looked at him wondering why he cared. But I didn't speak. Then he started to tell me how much he was going to give me for it. He said he would make sure that no one messed with me—I would be safe. I considered what he said, but I couldn't sell my watch—what would I use?

I was just standing there thinking about all the shit Ron was kicking out when another guy walked between us. He was carrying a bin full of clothes and water. He had on the same thing as Ron, except he wasn't wearing any socks. He also had a tattoo on his left shoulder that read "T" –that stood for Teddy, but to me he wasn't all that cute.

Turns out, Teddy and Ron were in the same cell together, cell one. They were the only two out during lock down because they were the runners on the block, and they did the cleaning on the block. Also in cell one was Bone—a player type cutie with green eyes and a smooth, well-muscled body. He and Teddy were cousins.

As I stood there talking to Ron and Teddy, I thought that with these two guys in here this might not be so bad. Plus, with these guys being the sanitation runners of the block, I knew they must have a lot of pull. It was so noisy in there. All I could hear were the people on the block locked down in their cells yelling and screaming like a bunch of mad men in a zoo. I felt very out of place.

"What cell are you in?" Ron asked.

"Fourteen," I told him. Then he informed me that I was being placed in a cell with a bunch of punk white boys and that they were corny as hell.

By that time the CO had brought me an empty gray box to store my clothes and other materials. I picked it up and headed to fourteen cell. Inmates were hollering and spitting through the bars. I was scared but not so scared that I couldn't keep walking. Fourteen cell was up a flight of stairs, and it smelled like shit. When the gate opened to let me in, I walked in on someone using the toilet. Staring me in my face were two white guys. They didn't say a word they just kept staring, almost like I wasn't human. I heard groaning from the toilet area, and was startled when a head popped up over the sheet. He too stared at me with a crazy look in his eyes. Then flushed the toilet, took the sheet down and came over to me without even washing his hands.

"Boy, I'm in here for murder, so you don't wanna fuck wit me!" I just looked at him as though he was crazy, because he was. I glanced around at the other white boys' faces. They just stood there, not smiling, not talking. I kept wondering if he was telling the truth about being in there for murder.

I dropped my box that contained my sheets, and ran back downstairs to where Ron was. A lot of people just kept looking at me. I guess they were aware that I was fresh meat on the block.

E-block was a block where younger people were placed. People my age, from eighteen to about twenty-five. But I could still see a few old heads on the block.

I told Ron that I did not want to stay in fourteen cell. In fact, I really wanted to stay in the cell with him because his cell had a TV, not to mention it seemed like a safer place to be. He looked at me with his big lips and said he was going to get me out of there. I wanted to say, "that's my baby," but I didn't.

He walked over to the guard's cage and told him, "He don't like white people and he don't want to stay in fourteen cell." Both the guard and I knew that Ron was lying, but it worked. Before I knew it, I had been given orders to move to nine cell. I kept staring at Ron, unable to keep my eyes off of him.

"Go get your stuff and take it to nine cell," he said with his enormous lips.

Joe, the toilet guy in fourteen cell, looked at me as I gripped up my box. He explained, "I'm not really in here for murder. I was just fuckin' wit you."

I didn't care. I still wanted out of there. I headed downstairs to nine cell. Soon as I walked through the door, this guy was smiling at me. He was grinning from ear to ear. He had a familiar face, I thought to myself, as he shook my hand. He acted like he didn't want to let my hand go. The cell was something like intake but it was much cleaner. No TV though. There was a single bed in the middle, instead of a bunk, with two sets of metal bunk beds against the walls. The guy was still standing in front of me smiling. He was wearing a pair of green boxers, no shirt, a long ass pair of socks rolled up all the way to his knees, and his slippers, which were known in the jail as shower shoes. He looked to be in his early thirties and had a low haircut with waves. He told me I looked familiar and asked if I was from West Philly.

"Yes," I replied.

"Well, that's where I seen you from," he said.

"Well, maybe," I replied.

He told me that his name was Nard.

"Well, the name Nard does not ring a bell," I said. Then I glanced over on the bottom bunk and saw my other cellmate, Montez, who was my age. His hair was nappy and he had a big nose. He reminded me of that old cartoon character "Mr. Bogus." I said hello, then gazed at the bunk where I was going to be sleeping. I took the sheets out of my box to make up the bunk, which was on top of Nard's. Ron came pass the cell and asked if I was okay. I told him I was cool. Ron lied and told Nard and Montez that I was his cousin. He told them no one better fuck with me. After I finished the bed I went to the doorway of the cell and looked around. I saw all sorts of people, even folks I used to go to school with. I headed out on the block toward the dayroom where the TV was. I sat on top of one of the stone tables to watch the *Moesha* show, when I realized a lot of people were staring at me. It made me uncomfortable, so I headed upstairs just to explore the place. When I walked by eleven cell I heard someone call me.

"Yo, come here!" I walked over and saw a dark-skinned boy with a bald head, maybe 18 years old. His name was Icon, not his real name, just the name he used.

"How much was your watch?" he asked. I told him I didn't know, it was a gift. Then he started telling me that he raps in New York somewhere. He had a nice muscular build with deep dark brown eyes--cute in a Michael Jordan sort of way. He passed me a commissary sheet and told me to pick out two of anything I wanted in exchange for my watch. I told him I would be right back. I went downstairs to where Ron was and sat down. He was playing cards in the dayroom with a cigarette hanging from his mouth.

"Some guy wants to buy my watch," I whispered in his ear.

"Get ten bags of chips and two packs of cigarettes," he replied. I didn't think that was a very high price, but Icon did. Although I came in with only sixty-four cents in my pocket, I wasn't about to sell my watch. It was nice, that's why I stole it. Anyway, I was not pressed for money, but I was starving. For the time being, I kept it.

I don't remember being this hungry ever before. I headed back to the dayroom to zone out on some TV, but realized that everyone was either staring at my watch or my boots. I was scared as shit. I wasn't entirely sure that if I were to get into something, Ron would have my back. I hoped Ron would cover for me. As I headed back to my cell I walked pass a lot of people playing chess, cards, and just standing around smoking. Montez and Nard were in the cell when I got there. Then, a tall dark crazy man entered. He was skinny and looked like he was about fifty years old. Larry was his name, but everyone called him "Old Head." I was surprised to know that I had to sleep in the same cell as him, in fact, mad.

I looked at Nard, "*Is he in this cell too?*" Nard nodded yes.

Of course I knew this was just something I'd have to live with. I tried to calm down, but I didn't know what this person was capable of. He walked around like he had a crook in his neck, almost like his neck was broken. As time went on I got used to him, and vice versa. He even taught me how to hold my hands in case I ever got into a fight. He would get agitated when he didn't take his medicine.

It was nice holding conversations with Montez, but at times he would act so dumb. All Nard talked about was how he used to be a credit card pickpocket. That's it. That's all he would talk about, day in and day out.

My first day there I sat at the guards' cage until it was time for lock down. It was eleven o' clock at night and once we heard that long whistle from the CO, it was time to head to our cells. My first night on E-block I slept good. I was snuggled up under a nice warm county blanket, and the heat was right over the top of my head. I slept with my clothes and boots on. I still hadn't taken a shower or brushed my teeth in five days. What was I to do? I was not getting in that nasty shower. I would be helpless in there, and I had no intention of getting fucked in the shower.

I lay on the top bunk and dreamed about someone that I had a crush on for a long time. I'm sure I was smiling as I dreamed, wishing that person would come rescue me from this hellhole. It seemed like the middle of the night when I heard the 6:00 a.m. whistle blow.

"Bottom tier, chow up!" called the CO. That was us. I heard the loud roar of the bottom tier's gate opening. I jumped down from the bunk and grabbed my plastic cup and the spoon. I proceeded out the door, with Nard following right behind. We all walked to the cafeteria, which seated about one hundred people. The line was very long and I was at the end. That particular morning they were serving shit on a shingle, the nickname for turkey sausage in creamed gravy. I didn't eat any of it. I gave it to Montez then went back to the block. No shower for the last few days was beginning to wear on me. The stubble on my face was itching like crazy. I was missing home a lot, but I was determined not to cry about it. I'd about reached my limit with Nard, always talking about how much money he used to take from rich white folks, how he and his wife were living it good off him being a pick-pocket. The same shit everyday—it was getting boring.

I spoke with my mother and the rest of my family. Everyone seemed very disappointed about my situation, but I imagined they all expected this much from me. I asked my mom to send me a television, but that was kind of hard since she was in the process of moving. I was bored. My only reading material was *Waiting to Exhale,* not that interesting since I'd already seen the movie several times.

I got used to going to the bathroom in front of Nard, even though there were times he would try to look over the sheet when I was taking a dump. My first weekend, I finally took a shower, after I sold Icon my watch for two pairs of socks, a pair of gym shorts, two t-shirts, and a pair of boxer shorts. I needed them clothes bad because I did not want to put my old clothes back on. I asked Montez and his friend Nate to stand outside of the shower because I didn't want anyone attacking me.

I was growing accustomed to being in the cell with Nard, Montez, and Old Head. I just didn't like Nard tapping me on my ass all the time. At one point the CO saw him and told him to stop. Montez's friend Nate was cool. He called himself a player. He loved girls. He was fine, too fine for me to even have a crush on him. He'd come by the cell every now and then to see Montez. He was cool with me.

I spoke to my mother throughout that first week. I wanted her to come visit me on Wednesday, but she said she'd come Saturday, although she didn't make it until Sunday.

Ron and Teddy almost seemed like my personal bodyguards. They loved me and I loved them. Teddy's cousin Bone seemed fond of me also. They knew I was a con artist and liked messing me up in my game. They felt like big brothers to me. Bone and I would have nice conversations about different things, such as each other's home life and what it was like when I realized I was gay. In fact, my being gay seemed like the number one question floating through everyone's mind.

Weeks went by and Old Head had to move out of the cell and on to another block because he was getting too crazy to stay in there with me. He started doing things like walking around the cell naked and then would come up behind me and rub his dick against my ass! I took his bed in the middle, between Nard and Montez. The new person that came in to replace Old Head was quite a character; he was fat, tall, and brown-skinned with lots of hair on his head. He kind of looked like Harry, from the television show *Harry and the Henderson's.* I was just glad that we got rid of Old Head. He had gotten so out of hand he had threatened to kill me.

I sold my boots to someone in the cell across from ours. I was really hungry and needed something to eat bad. They went for ten bags of chips, four Snicker bars, ten packs of Oodles of Noodles, and two packs of Kool-Aid. I didn't need the boots anyway. It wasn't like I had anywhere to go. I just walked around the jail in shower shoes.

Vince, was the name of our new cellmate. Besides sleeping a lot, he was crazy as hell. He'd walk around wearing a pair of tight thermal underwear. His toenails looked like claws. This big-ass dumb muthafucka with his crusty ass feet was always talking about how he could see a little man in the ceiling. The nurse had to come by every night to give him his medicine, just like Old Head. The only thing I missed about Old Head was the way we used to sit up half the night singing old songs that he didn't think I knew because of my young age.

Being in a cell with folks who were not normal was beginning to wear on me. One night Vince got horny and showed me his little dick print through his raggedy ass thermals, which was disgusting. Right about then I was really starting to miss home. I started to get more and more depressed. During some of my down times I wrote letters— to my mother and my brother, and I even kept a journal. I needed one in this crazy ass place. There was no peace of mind in nine cell. I had no one to talk to. It was always noisy and there was nowhere for me to go. I prayed that this would change soon, that I would get out, but it was no use.

My birthday came, and my mother came to see me, bearing a fifty-dollar money order. I sure needed it, mostly for new underwear. I only had three pair, and two of those came from my watch trade with Icon. Being out on a visit with my mother was cool. I so wanted to go home with her. She prayed for me and gave me focus, helping me stay strong. Of course she told me she loved me but that didn't carry far behind these brick walls. There was nothing I could do, but sit and wait. Neither of us knew when my court date was. I bought a notepad from the commissary along with a lot of food—more Oodles of Noodles, as well as nachos, cheese curls, candy bars, popcorn, and juice (powdered juice). All of this in an effort to satisfy my nighttime hunger pains.

Everyone on the block seemed to be my enemy. I didn't know why, since I didn't do anything to anybody. Maybe because I was paying too much attention to Teddy, Ron, and Bone. I was with them more than with my own cellmates. I really liked Bone, even though I still had a crush on Ron. I would watch Ron while he was in his cell lying on his bed or when he walked through the block in his boxers with his dick swinging back and forth. He would go around the block telling everyone that I was his bitch—I told him to stop. Then he would ask me if I wanted to go in the shower and I'd tell him no, although he knew I really wanted to.

There were about five people on E-block that I thought were cute. I even thought Butta was cute, despite his nasty-ass attitude. Butta was in three cell. He was short, light-skinned with a nice grade of hair and his feet were acceptable. Some nights I would sit in my cell and look over at three cell and watch him pull out his dick and take a piss.

I'd been in for about three weeks and was tired of living this life.

Around this time I was getting ready to go to court. Yes, my court date had come and I was so ready to go home. I wore Montez's boots, greased my face, and waited in outtake for my name to be called.

I was so looking forward to seeing my mother and being outside. I was handcuffed. As I walked outside I sniffed the fresh air. The breeze was nice and cool as they loaded us onto the prison van.

My mom was at the courthouse. Boy, I was glad to see her. I was led to a room in the back where I had to consult with a bail bondsman and a public defender. I spoke to them and figured there was nothing to this—I would be able to get out soon. I walked into the courtroom and sat down. The handcuffs were so tight around my wrists I couldn't move that much. I sat there while the judge approached the bench. I could feel my mom staring at me in the back. The judge announced that my bail was dropped to one dollar.

"One dollar!" I yelled out to my mother. I knew I could pay that. The public defender, however, made me aware that I still had the detainer and I was going nowhere with that. The only way I was getting out of there on that one-dollar bail was if my probation officer would be kind enough to lift the detainer. I got up, turned around, looked at my mother, and smiled. I felt certain I'd be going home soon. They carried me straight to the back after it was over, and then the sheriff escorted me back to the prison van. I could see my mother getting into her car and driving off. God, how I wished I was in the car with her.

I walked back into the prison. I felt used to the place and was not nearly as anxious as I used to be. I told Nard and Montez what the outcome was. They weren't surprised and didn't think I'd be getting out anytime soon.

"Man if you was a girl, I'd fuck the shit out of you," Montez said one night, as we listened to the rain hitting the bars on the window. Sitting on the bed I looked around the cell. Everyone was asleep. I got up and walked over to his bed and sat down beside him.

"Are you scared?" I asked. He told me that he wasn't.

"Its just too many people are watching. Somebody's always watching," he said. I looked down at him to see if he was hard, he wasn't. Then I yanked at the top of his boxers just enough to feel all of his pubic hairs and the top of his dick. By that time my hormones were blazing. Then I looked up at his nappy hair and his big nose and asked if he wanted to talk.

He just lit up a cigarette and started puffing. I just went over to my bed, lay down, and went to sleep. When Montez lit up his cigarette it made me think about when Old Head used to walk around the cell picking up old cigarette butts to smoke them.

A lot of people loved picking on me for no reason. I never did anything to anybody around there, but I had to keep in mind where I was. These people were not kind and loving, especially B-Real. B-Real was big and black. He resembled a whale. Everyday he would take time just to mess with me by slapping me across the face or touching my butt and calling me "sweet ass." It was horrible. It got so bad, Ron told him he would pay him off if he would just leave me alone. After awhile I began to notice that Ron was becoming quite fond of my cousin Carmen. I had a picture of her posted in my cell above my bed. Carmen was about my complexion and sort of resembled me, if not prettier, to most guys. I figured that was why he was being extra nice to me.

Sometimes I wanted to cry. I felt like the bitch of the block and everybody's punching bag. Inmates would often throw wet toilet paper rolls at me. I wanted to report B-Real to the authorities, but Ron talked me out of it. He talked to B-Real himself, and told him to chill. He was cool for a couple of days until he started his shit again. Even Nate got tired of B-Real's antics. There were times I thought B-Real was either going to rape me or kill me. He would lock me in my cell for hours until Ron came to my rescue. Nobody seemed like they wanted to help me. At night I would write to my probation officer, begging and pleading with her to lift the detainer so I could go home. I explained to the probation officer that I was very sad and that I needed out. I felt threatened and abused. I never got a response from her. I always talked to my mom about it. But, of course, there was nothing she could do for me. At night, I would walk around the block and make my way up to Nate's cell that was on the top tier in twelve cell. His cellmates were weird but cool, and best of all, his cell was quiet. It was a nice escape for me, away from all that noise of being downstairs and away from Nard's incessant theft stories. I always thought of Nate as being a really nice person. I had a good feeling about him. He was a bit of a recluse. Maybe he felt he had to remove himself from everyone because of his pretty looks. It felt like we were brothers; it was comfortable with him and his cellmates. They would sit back and get drunk off of the wine that they made themselves. Using fruit, sugar, bread, and water, they would let it ferment by the heater for a couple of weeks. I would have loved to be assigned to that cell, and that was the truth.

Being around Nard had its advantages. First off, he would never let anyone into the cell to take anything, and he spoke up when he felt as though things weren't going right. This was unlike Montez, who wouldn't say a thing if someone came into our cell and took something. Montez was jealous about me and Nate hanging together. He'd get into these sudden rages, wanting to hurt me. I wasn't all that scared of him because I knew Ron would cover me. Sometimes at night we'd lay in our beds and none of us would say a word to each other.

One night Nard called out my name. I looked over at him and he pulled the covers back and showed me his rock hard dick through the slit of his boxer shorts. I looked at him and he had the same big-ass smile on his face, just like the first time we met. I turned and continued to write my letter to the probation officer. This shit was getting out of hand. I didn't feel like I could take it anymore. I thought about killing myself, but what would happen after that? Would I ever see my mom again? Knowing how my life turned out was important to me. Would I ever get out of here? Clearly the probation officer didn't care. What if I got killed in here? As this tangle of thoughts ran through my head I held on to what my mother always told me, that a better day would soon come. God, I hoped that would be soon. As I tried to go to sleep, I stared at the wall, thinking of when I was free. It felt like I couldn't breathe. I needed air, more air than the window of nine cell was providing. I glanced over to the window and looked up at the stars. I never had a wish that was so intense, than the wish to go home. Somehow, I fell asleep.

The next morning I woke up to a lot of noise. I moved to the front of my cell to look to the top of the steps. There was Teddy sitting there holding a towel to his mouth. Suddenly someone came up to him and punched him in the back of his head. I ran back in the cell, put on my slippers, and ran up the other steps onto the top tier. Teddy then got up and started fighting back. All I could see was a gang of people jumping on him. I felt so bad about not being in a position to help him. Then I saw Ron and realized he was hitting Teddy! I couldn't believe it. My heart was pounding one hundred miles a minute. I can't fight a lick but I just had to help Teddy. Two of the people I cared about most were fighting each other. It just shocked me. Then I realized this was jail, and every man here was out for himself. I got scared. What if Ron decided to turn his back on me? I felt so sorry for Teddy as I saw him walk back to his cell. I wanted to cry. Instead, I felt this overwhelming tenderness toward him. A total crush. "Are you okay?" I asked him.

"Yeah, I'm cool," he answered. From that day on, I thought the world of Teddy. All the attention I had given to Ron was transferred to Teddy. I would do anything for him. If he asked me for anything, I would give it to him. It rained all that day. Teddy did not go to dinner. He didn't come out of his cell for two days.

I hated walking through the block, hearing everyone call me names, like "faggot boy" and "gay blade." Whenever the new inmates came on the block and found out I was gay, they would freak out. Nard was not helping. With all the animosity going on in our cell, it was decided that I should move out. I'd had enough when I was sitting on the toilet and Nard threw hot water on top of me. This led to a big water fight that flooded the whole cell. Turns out, I was headed to Nate's cell, which made both of us happy. Of course, Montez was upset because he had wanted to move in with Nate way before I did.

My new cellmates were Chowhall (we called him that because he loved to eat and was the ugliest person on the block); Roster or Breadman (because he loved to eat bread); and Leo. Chowhall was skinny and looked like an alien. He was about nineteen years old and rumor was, he wasn't getting out any time soon. Roster was sixty years old and made the wine all the time. He slept a lot of the time because of the medicine that he was on. He was a big man who loved his sweets. Leo, who was twenty-seven was from my neighborhood and seemed cool enough.

I stayed very close to Nate. We sometimes had arguments about who looked better. He always thought he looked good because of his beautiful dark skin. Because I told everyone I was getting a TV, Leo gave me the bottom bunk—it's one of the privileges. Things felt pretty cool. We put our blankets down on the floor to make it look like we had wall-to-wall carpet, and I put my box next to my bed for a nightstand. Our cell was called the "Bachelors Pad," and I loved it.

At night Nate and I enjoyed playing cards. I'd get so hungry. I couldn't wait until Friday when we got our commissary. I needed it bad. Nachos were usually the thing I had a taste for. Despite the better accommodations, I still wanted out of there. No matter how long I begged and pleaded to my probation officer, the detainer was not lifted.

Sometimes I would walk back downstairs to see Nard and Montez. We seemed to get along better when we weren't living with each other.

My arm was still hurting from B-Real punching me there and in my chest. Icon was in eleven cell, and would sometimes come by the door and watch B-Real hit me. But luckily Nate was not having that shit. Although he told B-Real not to come in the cell, B-Real came in anyway, and I was helpless. I was always helpless. I was sure I wouldn't survive this place.

My mother sent me a money order. I was glad. I could finally eat. I bought a rack of food, a lot of candy, and some cups to take chow with me out of the cafeteria. I always shared my food with my cellmates, including Leo, even though he never shared with me. I was aware that if I didn't share willingly, they would just help themselves.

One day B-Real came into my cell when I was sleep and told me, "No matter what Nate, Ron, or anyone says, if I want you, I will get you and nobody can stop me."

I looked at him and bravely snickered, but deep down inside, I knew he was telling the truth. Next door in eleven cell were a lot of young people that liked to pick on me, day in and day out. Icon was the only one that never really gave me any problems.

As April was finally coming to an end, it started to turn cold in the cell because the heater had been shut off. We took the blankets off of the floor, but that didn't help. I was freezing. I couldn't feel my toes. Some nights I had to put on Roster's big boots to keep warm.

Depression settled in during the early spring months. I felt too scared to take showers, and I continued to suffer physical and verbal abuse from fellow inmates. Sometimes I'd borrow someone's radio and would go back to my cell and lie down. I'd lie there with my ear pressed against the speaker listening to old sad tunes. I'd cry as I thought about all the things I was missing back home. It seemed like the more I cried, the more I hurt. Nate would come into the cell and ask me what was wrong and I'd tell him nothing. It seemed like I was the only one who was homesick. I guess I was the crazy one.

The people in eleven cell played entirely too much. They loved to throw water into my cell, especially when I was sleeping. And they loved body beating me. Those hits used to hurt.

My mother came to visit me on Easter Sunday. I felt so lonely. It was bright and sunny outside, but it was cold as hell in prison. My mother noticed that I was losing weight. I knew she was right because I was not eating. I craved fried chicken wings. My mother did have some good news; she said my television was on its way. I was happy to hear that.

It came about a week later. Everyone was happy. It was a brand new, black, thirteen-inch, color television. Now our bachelors pad was complete. Everybody wanted to come in the cell and watch, even Montez. I let him watch, along with a couple of other people that I didn't get along with, hoping to smooth things over. We all watched *Martin*. The TV was on all night.

At some point I realized that this television might not be a good thing. These muthafuckas were getting too happy with my shit! They were turning it on and off when they felt like it, and they where changing the channels, even when I was watching it! It seemed that Chowhall thought the TV was his. He'd curse me out and then turn to *Batman* without even asking me first. Leo would tell me he'd smack me in my mouth if I didn't let him watch the NBA play-offs. This was crazy.

Ron started in on me too. He'd call me names, come into the cell and rip the pictures of my cousin off the wall and take them around the block saying she was his girlfriend. B-Real still was not out of my life either. It was all so stressful. I wondered if this bullshit was ever going to end.

Teddy and Ron got fired from their positions as block runners. Ron was sent to pre-release and Teddy moved into seventeen cell, right across from twelve cell. Now that was just what I needed, a pretty face to look at while I was going through my trials and tribulations with these assholes from twelve cell (not including Roster and Nate). Roster, Nate, and I had a lot of fun cracking jokes on each other. When Nate went to court and found out the judge had put him on house arrest, I was happy for him. Although truly I didn't want him to leave. He was the only one I could talk to. I didn't like Nate as a boyfriend, but as a friend or a brother. I needed someone like him in my life while I was coping with my heartaches.

As Nate was packing up to go, he gave me his brush, I needed one. I was going to miss him. I was so sad. He also gave me his phone number, and I told him I was going to call when I got out.

The gate opened and the CO yelled "Nathan Brodus, discharged." I watched him as he went out to the gate and started shaking every one's hands that was in eleven cell. I turned around and continued watching television and the gate closed. I couldn't wait until the CO called my name: "Reginald Hall, discharged." Could not wait!

The cell was quiet. Leo came down from the top bunk and took Nate's bed, which was in the middle. I had the whole right side of the cell to myself. I put my clothesline up on my side and hung the few tee shirts I owned on it. The rest of the night was quiet. I wondered what Nate was doing.

"He's probably having fun," said Leo.

"I wish I was having fun," I said, and went to bed.

Now that Nate was gone, I felt I had no support. I made me a little knife out of a shaving razor. When B-Real came by to harass me I pulled it out on him. He just sauntered away and told the CO. About three o' clock that morning, several COs, along with the Gold Badge (the head CO), came to our cell and tore it apart looking for the razor. I had thrown it in the trash before lock down. We had to strip naked for them to check us to make sure that we weren't hiding anything in our private areas. It was so embarrassing and I was scared. They took all of our blankets and all of my razors. No more shaving. At least it wasn't too cold. I went to sleep, but not before we heard them tearing apart B-

Real's cell. We told the CO that he had the razor, so he and his cellmates had to do the same thing.

During the day there was nothing to do but watch television. Sometimes I'd walk around the block past Teddy's cell. He'd be lying in the bed watching TV with no shoes and no socks. Teddy had some cute ass feet. Sometimes I would go in his cell and sit and talk to him. Not too often though, I think he knew I liked him and I wasn't sure how comfortable he was with that.

Champs was what we called this guy from thirteen cell. He had a friend, Kareem. They were both older and were cool. Kareem was all about the Bible and was always trying to get me on the right track. We'd pray together, and sometimes that would make me feel better. I didn't have a real good sense as to what it meant to believe, but I had a feeling that reaching out to God would help.

J-Rock was in the same cell with Champs. At one point, when we were coming back from chow, he touched my butt and started laughing. I was mad as hell. I don't ever remember being so angry. When he realized he had offended me he apologized, and from then on we were close, so close that I started calling him my husband. J-Rock seemed too cool to be in prison, but I knew he must have done something to make it in here. J-Rock was no more than eighteen years old. He was brown-skinned, and while he wasn't the prettiest boy on the block, he wasn't the ugliest either. He had too many scars though (that shit turns me off), and his black toes also turned me the fuck off. Ninety percent of the inmates in here had black toes!

More and more people were coming in everyday. I knew by then that it must be about time for me to leave. They were coming in like running water. They'd see their homies and give them pounds and hugs like they were at a family reunion.

"Man, I'm gonna be in here for a long while," they'd shit with one another. Seeing this was sickening. How could anyone get comfortable with the idea of spending a lot of time here? I never really knew that I could last this long in jail. I was so tired of watching the same TV programs night after night. At times I would listen to the radio. The oldies but goodies came on every Sunday night. I couldn't help but crying some nights when a song came on that reminded me of how things used to be when I was free.

One Saturday morning, Roster found out he would be getting out for good behavior.

I was half asleep when the CO hollered up to the cell "Roster Clyde, discharged."

Breadman jumped up. He looked at Leo and me. I smiled (wishing it was me).

"Did he say what I think he said?"

"Yup," Leo said. "You leaving? Put your shoes on."

He looked at me while combing his hair. "I'm gonna call my wife," he said. Things hadn't been going very well between him and her, and she hadn't tried very hard to get him out of jail. He looked under his bed to get the rest of his things and then got up and walked out of the cell. I went to the gate and watched him walk down the steps. I knew he was happy that this was the last time he'd be walking down those steps. I turned around and looked at Chowhall. I was in shock that Roster left before me. Now I was in the cell with the two people who worked my nerves the most.

The rest of the day was boring. On weekends, we never ate lunch in the chowhall. Instead we had lunch on the blocks in our cells. Normally it was bologna on two pieces of soggy-ass bread, an orange, and a bag of potato chips. I hated bologna. I used to watch TV and watch everyone else eat. The electricity went out late that Saturday evening. Rain was pouring down outside. I stood by the window and looked at the rain for hours. Outside, trees were bending in the wind. I took my TV down from the windowsill, wrapped it up in a plastic trash bag, and placed it on the floor beside my bed. I could feel the rain beginning to come in through the window, but I didn't care. I loved feeling it on my face. It was so comforting.

Teddy, who was in the cell across from me, made it clear to Chowhall that he better have his food or the money Chowhall owed him on commissary day, or his ass was grass. Chowhall looked at me, scared. I wasn't too worried, I was too busy looking at the rain.

When the electricity goes out, all of the cells unlock, and the COs have to re-lock them manually, which they never do. So E-block was cut loose. At four o'clock in the morning people were out running around the block like it was daytime— throwing water, fighting and pissing into other people's cells that were still locked. Chowhall got up and took a shower. While he was in there, Leo stole his towel from off the metal banister. I stood up at the gate and watched for a while. I hated to get hurt or caught so I turned and finished watching the rain.

My mother came to visit on Memorial Day Weekend. It was nice of her to bring some money. I had been praying for a visitor. It sure seemed Kareem's guidance and teaching was paying off. I desperately needed to see a friendly face, and it being her was perfect. The visits felt like they were getting shorter and shorter. I hugged my mom and told her goodbye. I sat down in the chair waiting for the CO to escort me to the strip room.

I walked back onto the block, past the guards' cage, and on toward my cell. As I walked, it felt like I was walking through a crowd of drunks.

"Come here," someone called to me out of six cell. The cell was dark, so I didn't bother stopping, but someone grabbed my arm and pulled me in. I tried to resist but it was useless. All I could see were dark walls and about seven people looking at me. Two of them grabbed my arms, two grabbed my feet, and I fell to the floor, sobbing for help. More people continued to crowd the cell. Someone yanked my pants from the back and then grabbed them from the front. They were pulling and pulling. I saw J-Rock's face then, and I turned and glanced at the others. I couldn't believe this was happening. It was unreal. I tried not to scream because I didn't want to make more of a scene than was already going on. People were looking into the cell. I felt so embarrassed. By the time my pants got down to my ankles, everyone stopped. I jumped up and ran upstairs to my cell. My t-shirt was torn and everyone was staring at me, although they continued working at whatever they were doing. I stormed into the cell where Leo and Chowhall were watching TV.

"What happened?" Leo asked.

"They tried to rape me."

"Rape you? Who?"

"All of the guys that's downstairs."

"Now that shit is not right." Leo said that, but I knew he was not going to do anything to help me. Chowhall continued to watch TV. I sat on the bed trying to calm down. My heart was still beating at a fast pace. I changed my shirt. Then I got up and went back downstairs, passing Teddy on the stairs.

"What happened?" he asked. I just passed him and kept on going. I went in the dayroom towards the guards' cage. Everyone knew what I was going to do.

"They tried to rape me," I reported to the guard, and to my surprise he acted on it right away. I had to fill out a report and turn it in to the Gold Badge. When he called all of the people that were involved. I was told to go back to my cell. I did. I stayed there until the CO said that he was going to lock the block down, send me to intake, and send all the people that were involved to the hole. I sure as hell didn't want to go to intake. I knew if I went there, I was not going to be able to take my television and I'd be bored as hell. At this point more people kept coming to my cell asking me to let it go because they did not want to be locked down. I had already made up my mind to do just that when the CO took me downstairs to the dayroom.

He blew the whistle. "Lock em' up," he yelled. Everyone headed into their cells. I went to the dayroom where I saw J-Rock, someone named Black (he looked like a damn dinosaur, he was the one who helped Ron jump Teddy), a fat-ass boy named James, and a skinny boy named Doreen. I sat in the middle of James and Doreen. J-Rock was smiling at me and so was Black. Other boys at the end of the table were laughing also, but Doreen was crying. The Gold Badge sat across from me. I glanced around at all of their faces; J-Rock was the coolest of them all. I wasn't smiling, but the Gold Badge made it seem like it was all a joke. Everyone there stated that, in fact, it was a joke, that they didn't have any intentions of raping me. I looked at J-Rock's face and knew he was telling the truth. They all apologized, and that was that. We all got up from the table and started walking back towards the block.

"You want a hot dog?" J-Rock whispered in my ear and started laughing. I smiled at him. He was trying to smooth things over. I walked up the stairs and went to bed.

All of a sudden everyone was being nice to me. J-Rock started coming by my cell asking me if I needed anything (he was my husband...wasn't he?). Champs was starting to get pissed-off that Leo was taking advantage of my TV.

Chowhall did not have any money to pay Teddy come commissary day. Early that morning, Chowhall went to the guards' cage and asked the CO if he could be moved off the block. Late in the evening the gate to the cell opened.

"Where are you going, you owe me food?" yelled Teddy from seventeen cell. Chowhall played dumb and walked by Teddy.

"Hey Reg, did you know about this?" Teddy called out to me. Leo and I didn't know what was going on. I had to laugh. If Teddy was dumb enough to give Chowhall forty dollars worth of food, then he was dumber than I thought. So now it was just Leo and I in the cell.

I had been trying to get a job working in the kitchen for some time, and I was hoping that they would call me before the week was out. They didn't. It was starting to get hot. I didn't have a fan and E-block was not air-conditioned. I was hoping that Teddy would let me borrow his fan, but it was too late. His cousin Shannon had just come to the block and Shannon had the hots for me. I was trying to avoid him at all costs. Shannon was big, built, and black, (I mean crispy black) not my type at all.

"Let's go in the shower," he'd ask. "Are you scared?" I didn't know what to say or what to expect. He'd follow me around the block and hated that everyone called J-Rock my husband. He'd tell me not to go to dinner but to meet him in the shower instead. I wouldn't. One day I did asked him to buy me fifteen dollars worth of food from the commissary. He did. Then he asked me for a kiss. I kissed him on the cheek.

I was okay being in the cell with only Leo. He was cool. I didn't have to argue over my television. I could just lie in the bed and watch TV, and he would watch what I wanted. Champs, Kareem, and Shannon would come in the cell everyday to watch TV with me. I was cool with that. Leo kept quiet. He wouldn't say a thing. I guess cause he knew what Shannon might do to him.

By June, the walls were sweating and so was I. Teddy finally let me borrow his fan and we also got two new cellmates. They were terrible. Another nightmare.

Leo, along with the two new cellmates, John and Mike, all acted like they owned the TV. My head was a mess, all nappy and out of control. I needed a haircut bad. The two runners from H-block were barbers; they came by to cut our hair. To be a runner from H-block you had to work in the jail. I wanted to get there so bad. That was the only block that had air conditioning. My haircut looked all right, but it wasn't my normal cut. The guy that cut my hair was kind of cute. His name was Cash. I guess that's because he had a lot of money. He was a Muslim though, and I knew he wouldn't go for any faggot shit.

I could never watch what I wanted to watch on TV, and Leo was threatening me with physical violence. I was getting really scared. I didn't have anyone. I wasn't sure if Shannon would help me or not after I told him he wasn't my type. Somehow I convinced the guard to move me to thirteen cell with Champs and J-Rock. They were happy to hear that I wanted to move in the same cell with them.

When Leo heard that I was moving he was pissed. He cocked his hand back as if to punch me in my face, but he didn't. Everyone stared at us from their cells. Leo dragged my stuff out of the cell, yelling at me to get the fuck out. Of course my husband (J-Rock) was helping me carry my stuff, including my television. After moving that TV out, I was scared to even look Leo in the eye. Neither of us spoke. I knew that being in thirteen cell with Champs and J-Rock would be so much better. The basketball game was on, so of course I let Champs and J-Rock watch the game. Champs gave me the bottom bunk, so while they were watching the game I got myself situated. I put my clothesline on the bottom bunk, made my little nightstand with my box, and I was set. Eleven o'clock, it was time to lock the block down. Once again everyone was running around trying to get hot water for their Oodles of Noodles, and to get their last cup of water for the night.

I lay in the bed and watched *Martin* on TV, bored because all they were showing were reruns. I reached for my journal that I kept under my mattress. I was counting down the days before I went to court. I wrote a small entry in the book before we cut off the TV for the night. Champs turned off the light, and J-Rock called my name.

"Now that the light is off, you and J-Rock can get ya'll freak on!" Champs said from the top bunk. I smiled. J-Rock got up to take a piss. He turned around with his dick hanging. I was shocked to see that he had such a nice size. Then he started to shake the rest of the piss into the toilet. I was getting *hot.* I watched him until he got back in bed and got under the covers. I loved the way J-Rock took me under his wing. I felt very comforted around him, like I was really a part of him. He'd have these smoke parties and invite all his friends to the cell to smoke weed. He was always very kind to me, and it felt good knowing he had the connections to get most anything.

Shannon wasn't too crazy about me liking or being around J-Rock, or that J-Rock took up for me in any situation. Anyway Shannon started to get on my nerves. I hated that he was around me every minute of the day, or that he would stand there and stare at me while I slept. Thankfully the sheriffs came and got him because he had to serve the rest of his time upstate. That was a relief. Being in the cell was cool now. If I needed anything, J-Rock would give it to me, and all of the troubles I was having with Leo, J-Rock took care of. He made me laugh. One thing I didn't like was when we would play fight, because he hit hard as hell. Some mornings we'd all just lay in bed, not going down for breakfast. We'd sleep all morning, especially J-Rock; he loved sleeping until about one or two o'clock.

They respected me in that cell and it felt good.

I called my mom from time to time to see what was going on out in the world. The process was the same every time:

"Bell Atlantic has a collect call from-Reginald, at the Delaware County Prison. To refuse this call-hang up. To accept this call, do not use three-way or call waiting features or you will be disconnected. To accept this call, dial one now. Thank you." It was nice to keep up with the family news, although hearing it made me homesick. I had a cousin who graduated from junior high school, and a car had hit my brother, but he was okay. I'd talk to her for about a half-hour at a time, I didn't want to run up her phone bill too much.

One time, to pass the time, I watched J-rock comb his pubic hairs. That was a turn on for me. You know, a real man doing work. After I snapped out of my trance I turned toward the TV. J-Rock got up to change the channel. He had pulled his shorts down just enough to let his dick hang out over the elastic of his boxers. I just stared at his dick and watched his lovely hanging balls. I wished I had a camera.

"Why you looking at my dick?"

"Well, if you didn't want me to look, then why did you pull it out?" He smiled and then tucked it back in his boxers. I knew that J-Rock wanted me bad. I wanted him too, but my mind was still on Teddy.

Two days later I was getting ready for my sentencing date at court. I got a haircut and lotioned my face so I would look shiny clean and innocent. Everyone on the block, who cared, prayed for me. I even prayed for myself. Champs told me to walk in prayer and keep my mind focused on the Lord. Yeah, I guessed this was the best time for me to start believing. I tucked my undershirt into my pants and put on my brown shirt. Then I sat on the side of the bed and waited for the CO to call my name. Teddy was staring at me as I walked down the metal steps toward the dayroom. I got my pass from the guards' cage and through the gate I went. I walked rapidly through the chow hall down to outtake. About twenty other people had court that day. I was handcuffed to two other guys that were much, much older than me. When the CO opened the doors, I walked outside and took a deep breath—through my nose and out my mouth. I climbed into the van thinking I just might be home at this time tomorrow. When we arrived at the courthouse I was overwhelmed with the thought that my mother might be able to take me home. She was at the courthouse all right, but not to take me home.

I realized while sitting there with all the other inmates—their crude way of talking and their bad manners—throwing their cigarette butts on the floor—that I was starting to fit in. I didn't remember what it was like to be around civilized folk. It was a depressing thought. They finally called my name. I walked trough the long hallway with the sheriff holding on to my right arm. We walked upstairs and in to the courtroom. My mother was sitting in the back row. She was looking tired and confused, probably because it was now ten after three and my hearing was scheduled for nine this morning. The bailiff took the handcuffs off my hands and I stepped in front of the judge to plead guilty to the charges. I was found guilty and the case was dismissed. The sentence I received was time served; by then I'd been there three months. When all was said and done, however, I still had the detainer facing me, and so, back to prison I went.

After that court day, I was so depressed. I just felt like lying around in bed. I'd stare at the pictures that were stuck to the wall with toothpaste and think about old times. Would those times ever come again? Only God knew. I had a dream about God, that I was standing in front of him on judgment day, the rain falling down on my face while he considered my days in prison. The gates opened for me, I could hear their roar. Freedom was at hand. To my surprise, I woke up to find that the big roar was the prison gate being opened. I lifted my head up from the pillow and laid it back down, relieved but a little disappointed that my time had not yet come.

One day, when we were scheduled to see the counselor, I woke up early so I could get to his door before everyone else. I needed out of this place, so I was trying to get in touch with my probation officer to find out what was going on. But the counselor continued to be of no help. He told me my probation officer was not in her office and, in fact, was not going to be there for two weeks due to her vacation. I was suffocating in here. I knew that it was just a matter of time before someone would find my body lying in the bed not breathing.

Be strong, I counseled myself. I just wrote in my journal as often as I could. Writing about my thoughts helped me stay focused, to not get lost in the pit. It came as no surprise when someone stole my journal and passed it around to the whole block to read. This proved devastating for some of my relationships. Teddy found out that he was the love of my life, and it made him so upset that he stopped speaking to me and started to join in with everyone calling me names. I tried not to cry, but I couldn't help it. I called my mom. I knew there was nothing she could do, but at least I could feel her love for me. I hated this place. I felt Teddy looking at me out of the corner of his eye; calling me names across the hallway; spitting my way. I dared not look at him. My secrets were no longer secrets. Everyone knew. Everyone knew about me—what I do, what I like to do, and what I dreamed of doing, especially to Teddy.

J-Rock was silent for three days straight. Champs cracked jokes, but not meanly. With Kareem being down in pre-release it was just me and Champs praying together. I hated being called a "stinkin' bitch," but I really couldn't blame J-Rock for being mad. He had done more for me than Teddy ever had. Now I had to suffer the consequences.

The first time I caught Teddy's eye, sweat started pouring down the side of my face. He ran up to me and told me that he would fuck me up if I ever looked at him again.

Despite the stress, being on E-block was getting to be homey. I was getting used to it, running around on the block with the others and acting like a nut, playing cards, and learning card tricks. I was also spending more time with Icon. I never knew he had such sexy eyes. I was suspicious of some of the guys' sexual orientation, because when I'd touch their dicks they would rise. I was hot, and needed some lovin' bad, but I knew this was not the place for that.

J-Rock, his feelings still hurt, started beating on me. Boy did those hits hurt.

I never felt so alone. I was getting really annoyed with my probation officer and her extended vacation. It was hot and humid in E-block. I just lay across the bed and cried. I cried for my life. I cried for my body. I cried for my soul. Exhausted, I fell asleep. I needed to get away. J-Rock was starting to get on my nerves. He was acting like I was his enemy and I didn't like that at all. I'd be starving and he would say that he didn't have anything for me to eat. I wanted to leave this block bad. I knew the only way I could speed up the process of getting a job in the kitchen was for me to give the yellow shirt runner a pack of cigarettes. I didn't have any money on my books nor did I have any cigarettes, so at night when everyone was asleep, I went into J-Rock's gray box and stole a pack. Honestly, I regret doing this, but I felt I had no choice. I couldn't stay on that block any longer being treated the way I was.

The next morning I slipped the pack of cigarettes to the yellow shirt runner. He told me he would take care of everything.

Later that day I heard it, "Reginald, you're moving to H-block," someone yelled from the gate. I never thought the day would come where I'd go to the air-conditioned trailers. I wiped the sweat from my forehead and packed everything in my gray box. I was scheduled to move after dinner.

The block went to dinner. J-Rock was so quiet. Honestly, I really didn't want to leave him. After dinner I walked back in the cell and J-Rock looked at me, we both smiled. I looked at Champs and hugged him. I turned around to J-Rock who told me he didn't want me to go. The CO arrived and picked up my TV. He carried it out to the dayroom. J-Rock tossed a cup of water onto my shirt. I smiled. He smiled a fake smile. I shook his hand and told him I'd miss him. Then I walked out of the cell. The gate closed behind me. Teddy looked at me as I walked down the steps. I guess there'd be no goodbye dick for me.

H-block

I had asked the CO to help me with my TV because as I was leaving people were throwing water at me. This was common. I'm sure jealousy played a part. Despite being so completely relieved to get out of E-block, I knew I would miss it, at least some of the people. I was thinking about Champs, and the way he would walk around in his underwear as if he was superman. I had everything in my box, except my brush, which I had given to J-Rock-- something to remember me by. I passed by Butta on the way out. He was coming in from court. He was being discharged on that day and was quite happy. His bail was a dollar and he didn't have a detainer, so he was out.

The block runners that had taken the place of Ron and Teddy were in one cell, and they helped me with my box and television. They wanted me to give them my antenna because they had broken theirs. I said no, but of course they took their chances and tried to steal it anyway. I was happy to be on my way out of E-Block.

Walking to H-Block made me a little nervous. First I had to go through the chow hall, where another block was still having dinner. Everyone stared at me as I made my way through. Najee, the E-block runner, walked with me through a long hallway. At the end was a steel door that had to be buzzed opened. We walked down three flights of stairs. Soon as I approached the doors, a blast of cold air hit my face. It felt good, real good.

I walked down the metal steps and into the trailer. It really was a trailer, attached to the jail. I'd never seen anything like it. The guards' cage was inside a real office. It was cool, quiet, and relaxed. I sat my box down and Najee sat the television down before returning to E-Block. I felt relieved. No more heat. No more sweat. In fact, it was downright cold. I walked through the dayroom that served the eight trailers. I was assigned to four trailer, which was the trailer for morning kitchen. I opened the door to go in and saw that the floor and the walls were made of tin. It almost felt like I wasn't in jail anymore. There were no cells, no bars, and people were just walking around like they were on the street, listening to walkmans, playing cards, gambling, and smoking. There were ten metal bunk beds to a trailer. I was on the top. I hated to be on the top. I saw a couple of people that used to be on E-Block, even this one boy that moved to H-Block because B-Real kept messing with him—chewing up toilet tissue and spitting in his face. This place was amazing. The showers were all the way in the back, along with the toilets. It was quiet in my trailer because people were resting so they could get up at one o'clock in the morning to go to work. After I made my bed I toured the rest of the trailer. I loved that I could take a shower anytime I wanted. The beds had little shelves built in for those who had a television. My television wouldn't play right though because I needed a cable cord. Antennas wouldn't work right with all the metal in there.

Someone opened the door; a slim guy, light-skinned, and nicely groomed with a mustache and smooth goatee. I recognized him from when he'd visit E-block to play cards. Nasir was his name and saying hello was my game. He was P-H-Y-N-E!

"Do you have a cable cord I can use?" Anything to start a conversation.

"No, but I can find you one," he replied. I didn't believe him, but I was wrong. As he talked to me, I kept staring at his short, dark, wavy hair. I was about to explode if he didn't kiss me. He didn't. I didn't need to be out of jail; those pink lips could just set me free.

"Yeah, I found you a cord, but you have to give me a pack." I should have known. If you want anything from anybody in this jail you have to give up at least one pack of cigarettes.

"I don't have any cigarettes," I told him. I stood there with a sad puppy dog look on my face. He gave in. He told me to follow him to eight trailer where he stayed. Eight trailer housed p.m. sanitation workers. He took me to his bunk where I pulled up a chair next to him. He sat down on the bed and handed me the cable cord. I wondered if he was *the* one. I could smell the powder scent that was coming from his bed. This trailer was much cleaner than four trailer and, of course, I wanted to move in. He sat right in front of me and smiled, I smiled to. I knew I wasn't looking my best; I definitely needed a haircut. I said a silent prayer, hoping that he was the one for me.

"How old are you?" he asked.

"Eighteen," I squeaked in one of my preteen voices. I asked him how long he'd been in the prison. He told me he'd been in for a year and should be getting out in a few months. He turned on the radio. Alexander O'Neal's *Sunshine* was on.

"This is my jam!" I said excitedly. Nasir smiled and turned up the volume, watching me as I started to sing. Then he started flipping through the channels on his TV, using a remote! These people lived in luxury. It was a shame that all the other blocks couldn't be like this one. I sat there day dreaming about the fact that that song came on while I was sitting next to the cutest guy in the jail (besides Teddy). I continued to mumble the words to the song until it was finished. Then I glanced over at another guy who was laid out watching his own television, it was Radii, another runner for the jail. He was cool, down-to-earth, and liked to play a lot. He started acting like Nasir's guard dog. He got up, came over to me, and started checking me out from top to bottom. He was so funny.

"Radii plays a lot," Nasir said smiling. As he flipped through the channels he told me he was from Chester. Then he started showing me all these pictures of his family, friends, and girls he used to fuck. I even came across some pictures of Teddy and his girlfriend, Butta and his brother, and Bone and his cousin! You could tell that Chester was a small town, because everyone knew each other. I thought to myself, all this because I asked for a cable cord. He just sat there looking *so* cute.

Cash, the barber, came into the trailer. He looked at me and smiled. He asked when I came to H-block. I told him just that day, and that I was going to work in the kitchen. He patted me on the back of the head like I was some type of dog. He asked Nasir for a bag of nachos.

"When are you gonna cut my hair?" I asked.

"When are you gonna give me some fuckin' money?" he asked.

"Man cut his hair!" yelled Nasir.

I looked at him and thought, "Yeah that's right, take up fo' yo' bitch."

Nasir gave him the nachos, and then Cash left. It was just Nasir and me, once again, alone. I wanted to kiss him so bad, but then the eleven o'clock whistle blew; time to lock up. I headed back to four trailer after telling him I'd see him tomorrow. He smiled and nodded okay. I loved every minute of it. At my trailer I went about hooking up my TV. I still couldn't get good reception. I just turned it off and went to bed. I prayed, thanking God for removing me from E-block and sending me to H-block. I knew there was a reason for everything, that there must be a reason for me being here. I hoped Nasir was the reason.

About two hours after I fell asleep the lights slammed on. They were very bright, shining right in my face up there on the top bunk.

The CO came in the trailer yelling to the kitchen workers, "It's time to get up, let's go!" Four times he repeated that. Everyone got up and started to get dressed. I was given a pair of white pants and a white shirt. Man, was I tired. Below my bunk was an older guy with glasses named Sherman. He kind of looked like Herman Munster. In the bunk in front of ours was a guy named Monty. He was skinny and kind of cute. He looked like the little dog off the Taco Bell commercials. Across from my bunk was Donnie, who was real dark, missing his two front teeth, and all of his toenails were black. Monty was in the bunk below Rahim. Rahim and I had been in middle school together. In front of them was Fattman, and he was a *fat man*. He was kind of cute, in a teddy bear kind of way. Above him was the one and only James, a real class clown. In front of him was Tony, a big man, lots of muscles; he used to take steroids. He was black, bald, and very aggressive. Across from Jamie was Marshal who had done eight years and was hoping he'd be released that year. Above Marshal was a white man named Joe. As far as I could see, Joe was an educated fool.

When I finished getting dressed I admired my uniform and my sneakers—given to me by Shannon before he went upstate. I was so used to seeing myself in those browns that this was a nice change. Then we got our nametags and proceeded upstairs to the kitchen.

Mary was the kitchen supervisor. She was a big girl with a loud mouth and an attitude that reminded me of my aunt.

That just made me all the more homesick. Mr. Perry was a supervisor also. He was calmer. He was probably in his mid-fifties. He didn't really care what we did in the kitchen as long as the work got done. Bud was the head supervisor. Any concerns or problems were reported to him. He was quite old, but he could get around when he needed to. He talked with a strong southern accent; listening to him made me laugh.

My first day in the kitchen had me working the French toast line. That's when I met Butler. A man in his late forties, he was real cool with me, and we grew quite fond of each other. He was always there when I needed someone to talk to, and vice versa. He worked next to me on the front line passing out milk to the inmates. He was real black and had a big belly; he looked like about nine months pregnant. During my time in the kitchen he helped keep me out of trouble, especially when Mary would yell at me and I wanted to yell back. But I didn't want to go back to E-Block so I didn't say a word. We were only making about thirty-five cents an hour and the work was very stressful and hard. It was so hot in there. We worked from 2:00 a.m. to 10:00

a.m. That first day I was tired. I couldn't wait to get into bed. We served all the blocks. I liked it when E-Block came in, especially when J-Rock and Champs came through the line. I'd give them extra pieces of food. Fuck everyone else. That first day, Teddy stuck his head through the window asking me for shit. I told him to get 'outta my face and he called me a bitch. I laughed, so did Butler. After our shift was over, I went back downstairs to the trailers. I was so glad to get back in the cool air. I took a shower, put on my shorts, a t-shirt and a pair of ankle socks. The only thing I didn't like about these showers was cold air blowing on my bare ass.

I didn't like working in the kitchen at all, but didn't want to go back on that hot ass block. I asked the counselor if I could I get my job changed. He told me no.

It rained and rained. The power went out—which included the air conditioning. We were sweating in the trailer. It felt like we were in a sardine can. I just lay on the top bunk thinking about Nasir. Did he forget about me or what? I hadn't seen him all day. I fell asleep.

Cash came in and told me he was ready to cut my hair. By then the power had come back on.

I sat there, watching loudmouth James and Fattman crack jokes on one another. Monty and Rahim were still asleep. Marshal was on the toilet as usual. I noticed that I wasn't the only homosexual on H-Block. Peanut was the other guy's name, and he had the biggest head. He was cool though. It was fun hanging around with him and sharing who our crushes were with each other.

The jokes that day had to do with the kitchen staff, Mary especially. I guess Mary had a crush on James, who was joking, telling us this story, "I was in the bathroom taking a shit and Mary kept banging on the door, saying 'come out,' and if I don't then she was gonna come in there. I told her,' you bring yo' big ass in this bathroom if you want to. I'll bust yo' ass right over this sink!"

Then James would imitate Bud's voice, "What's all this bologna doing on this damn floor? Put this shit back in the freezer!"

Then he'd do Mr. Perry, "Ya'll stealing again huh?"

The entire trailer started laughing and couldn't stop. James offered me non-stop laughter with all his jokes. We got to be very close. Everyone thought we were a couple. For once I wished "everyone" would couple me up with someone I could couple with! Nasir wasn't coming down to see me that much. The folks in his trailer started making fun of the way I walked and talked. I guess they started to tease Nasir about being around me so he stopped coming by. He even started telling people that he was only talking to me because he wanted me to hook him up with my cousin. It didn't matter much to me anyway, ever since I saw his feet. They were nice, except on his big toe there was a black toenail.

Shyheed, from eight trailer, was the coolest. He too liked the way my cousin looked, and I hoped they could get hooked up, but he also wanted me to be his friend. Shyheed was kind of thick, just the way my cousin liked them. He was dark and cute, with curly hair that sat on the top of his head. He didn't care what people thought about him talking to me. He'd come to four trailer to check on me everyday. I kind of had a slight crush on him. But really I liked him as a brother; we even told people on other blocks that we were brothers. It was nice; he didn't let anybody fuck with me.

The counselor finally switched my bunk to a bottom bunk. This wasn't like E-block where you could just move to the bottom bunk; here you had to be assigned. A lot of things were very different here. People had real pajamas and bathrobes and they could wear their street clothes. Smoking weed was pretty common too, even in front of the COs. I found out when my new court date was, so I was just waiting. James and I had the same probation officer, so he was waiting too. We were both in there for the same thing. Him and Donnie got locked up together for using stolen credit cards at a department store. Everyone could tell that James and Donnie were very close because they used to talk about each other's mothers and you know, no one likes for their mother to be talked about.

The summertime was just lingering on. All I could do was think about home. I'd stare at myself in the mirror for hours making funny faces at myself, crying or laughing. I wondered what was going on out in the world. I wasn't getting enough information. All I could do was pray.

I maintained the job working in the kitchen by putting up with Mary's fat ass.

"James?" She loved calling his name with her loud ass mouth. She used to think that I liked James, even though I didn't, I just liked his company.

"When you gonna do my hair?" James always asked me. I did his hair in braids, and Mary hated that. It took me a while to figure out why she was always trying to fire me from the kitchen. I didn't want James, not at all. Realizing that working the kitchen wouldn't last as long as she was there, I decided to do my best and stick it out as long as I could. Although I had constant thoughts of suicide, that didn't stop me from seeing if I could find someone in that damned place who would at least give me some.

To keep my sanity, I'd sing real loud on the front line, just to make Mary mad. She'd look at me with her eyes crossed and then look at James while he laughed his ass off. I didn't give a fuck. I was hot, tired, and that prison job wasn't paying shit. Thirty-five cents an hour just wasn't enough, and I was tired of this old man named Country that wanted to do it to me. The only good thing about the kitchen was that we got to eat anything we wanted. I finally started to put on a few pounds. Stealing food everyday from the kitchen and taking it down to the trailers was nice. Sometimes we had to sneak the food in through a bag of ice because the CO would check it.

While we were in this jail, there was a new jail being made right across from the old one. Rumor was we were all going to move to it. Moving to that new place would be a nightmare. Rules included no smoking and no leaving the block. Everything was done on the block: the gym, the chow hall, the basketball courts, etc. And no more stealing food: no more taking lettuce, tomatoes, pickles, and cold cuts so we could make our own sandwiches. Mr. Perry always said there was more food on H-Block than there was in the kitchen. Being in the trailers had its advantages but I wished to God that I could click my heals three times and go home.

About eighty-five percent of the people in the trailers were Muslim. On H-block they would bow down on their colorful rugs, pray, and sing to Allah. Cash was Muslim. I had him cut my hair one day.

"Are you gay?" he asked.

I was shocked to hear that coming from him. He stared into my eyes and said, "Has anyone ever told you that you have some pretty ass lips?"

I didn't know whether to laugh or just look at him and ask him to repeat the question. Then, as he's shaping up my neckline he puts his hard dick on my back! I would never think that Cash would ever think of me in this way. Luckily, before I could say anything, he wrapped it up by saying that he would talk to me later.

My hair was looking sharp. I walked through my trailer and peeped out the corner of my eye to see Nasir standing to my right. I had the feeling he was trying to brush me off so I kept walking as if I didn't see him. I could still remember when he called me a faggot when he thought I was asleep. Although he was looking cuter everyday, I tried to keep my composure when he would walk through the trailer with his buddy Jawan. Jawan looked pretty young for his age. I think he was about nineteen. He was dark-skinned, kind of cute, especially when his hair was neatly trimmed. He couldn't stand gay people. I hated when those two hung together because they'd stare at me and crack jokes about me. One night I asked God to show me a sign to see if Nasir was the one for me. I guess I got my sign when I saw him go to the shower one day barefoot. One foot looked pretty as hell, then on the other there was a black toe. I was crushed. Well, life must go on.

I tried to get all the advice I could from the older crowd. We all vowed that we would never come back here again.

One day I was watching TV, when James blurted out "I can't take this shit no more!" I mean he said it as if he was gonna blow the roof off.

I sat and talked to Tony for hours, asking him questions about how he came to prison and what would he do if he got out. It was nice to pass the time this way. I just loved his stories and poems, including this one:

One bright sunny day, in the middle of the night
Two dead boys got up to fight
Back-to-back, they face each other
Took their swords and shot one another
The deaf police officer heard the noise

Came and shot the two dead boys
And if you don't believe this lie is true
Ask the blind man he saw it too.

Waking up at one thirty in the morning was a bitch. I was tired as hell when those lights would shine in my face. Shaking the sleep out of my bones just to work in some fuckin' kitchen. I hated it. I was miserable and I felt as though I was going to explode. I called my mom, she was trying to help me stay focused, telling me I would make it out of there. When? I couldn't handle this much longer. After everyone put their clothes on, we'd walk upstairs and through the long hallway. It made me feel kind of special like I was going on stage at a rap concert. But in reality I was headed to a filthy ass kitchen where I only made thirty-five cents an hour. I couldn't complain though because I had prayed to God that he relieve me from that hot E-block, and he did.

D-block was the block with all the murderers and rapists on it. They were locked down for twenty-two hours and out for recreation for only two. This one, and JHU, the juvenile block for the people that were seventeen and younger, were the only blocks that didn't come to the chow hall to eat. Instead, we had to set up their trays and James would deliver their food.

Mary and I still had our problems. She really thought I wanted James. However, she was cool enough to let my mother know when I had a sudden unplanned court date. I didn't know I had court on that particular day, and when my name was called I was shocked. I looked at Mary, and she looked at me. The first thought that came to my mind was did my mother know I had court and forgot to tell me? All I knew is that if they call your name, you should go. I went. Back down through outtake again. Turns out, it was all a mistake and I didn't have a court day, but no one told my mother. She waited there all day.

Now on to this old guy named Country. He had the worst yuck mouth I ever saw. Every other tooth was missing. He looked at me like I was a piece of steak at his last supper. I smiled because it made me laugh inside, him thinking he was getting a piece of this ass. I mean ugly, an ugly-ass nigga. He was so skinny, old, with scraggly gray hair on his face. I will admit, I asked him for plenty of favors at different times, but I had no intention of giving him anything in return. One time, during a break, Country followed me out to the hallway. I just sat there looking like an innocent schoolgirl talking to the child molesting principle. I wasn't scared of him, not by a long shot. I know how to deal with trash. He launched into his story, telling me about his family, and more shit that I didn't want to hear. After feeding me the bullshit, he asked if he could make love to me. Of course I said no. Then he continued telling me how he had a big dick, etc.

God, I needed to get home. It seemed the gates of hell couldn't be half as bad as being in here. I swallowed some of Fattman's pills to relieve me from the depression I was having, but it didn't work. The side effects were a muthafucka. I just wanted to be knocked out, but when I woke up I had a terrible stomachache and couldn't shit or vomit. I lay in my bed holding my stomach praying to die. Eventually I fell back to sleep. I woke up to find Cash sitting on the side of my bed shaking me. I woke up in a daze hoping that I was some place else.

"Wassup?" he asked.

I looked at him as if he had antlers growing from his head. Did he not know that I felt like shit and all I wanted to do was go home, in the worst way? All these niggas in this fuckin' prison can do is eat, sleep, and shit.

"Nothing, I just got a lil' headache," I replied. Man, this boy talked for hours. He was telling me that he liked me for sometime, but of course I played hard to get. I just lay there and listened to everything he had to say. I thought he was cute, but he was too buff.

"So when can I hit that?" he asked, looking at the print of my ass through the covers.

"Never!" was my answer. Then I started smiling, asking him if wanted to go all the way. He asked to feel me and I told him no, I wasn't frontin'. The rest of the trailer folks were asleep, or so I thought. Then James popped his head up. Cash took off, telling me he'd talk to me later. I got up from my bed. James and I walked out of the trailer. We were laughing as I headed toward the showers.

All that day I slept. I was madly depressed and itching to know what was going on out in the world. I grabbed my radio and tuned it to 105.3 WDAS, where I found Brian McKnight's *Anytime* playing. I just lay there and sang along. I sang 'til the tears came. I thought about being at home with my mom and my brothers, and my room at home. By then my eyes were like a swimming pool. I needed that cry. I looked around the trailer; no one was in there but me. They were all in the dayroom watching the movie *Friday*. I loved that movie but I just couldn't stand seeing something so funny in a place as depressing as this.

It wasn't 'til a quarter of ten when my damn roommates began shuffling in. Huh! The movie must be over. I got up, put on my shower shoes, walked over to the payphone and called my cousin. That phone was broken, meaning I could call anyone's house collect. (Normally I could only call my mom, since her number was in the system). I talked, and talked, and talked: to my mother, my aunts, my cousins, my brothers, my grandparents, and my best friends. I had a great time on the phone right up until CO Brown blew the whistle. I placed the receiver on the hook with a smile, thanking the Lord for my brighter day. I went back into my trailer and lie down with a heart on the mend. I was so thankful I got to speak with all the people I cared about and that they were happy to hear from me.

Despite the liberties of H-block, I was getting more depressed. My one saving grace was my relationship with CO Brown. He was like a father to me, and I will always love him for that. He made me feel comfortable. He'd put in a lot of overtime and tell me he was always there for me. My heart was so at ease when he was on duty. Even so, I knew I was down when the Fourth of July came around and I didn't even step outside for yard out. I don't think I ever cried so much in my life. I thought about everyone on the outside celebrating while I was on lock down. I couldn't stand it. If only I could find a piece of rope. Maybe the sheets would work. I tied one end of the sheet into a knot and then proceeded to wrap it around my neck. I tied the other end to the top bunk. I wanted my life to end. It just so happened that Butler was passing through in the hallway, coming to check on me. He grabbed me and prayed for me as I fell to the floor. Happy Fourth of July to me.

I had an invitation to visit Cash at his trailer at a certain time. Maybe I'd do something or maybe I wouldn't. I *was* looking cute. I had just gotten my hair cut and my face was just as bright as the sun. I walked out of my trailer and smiled at CO Brown as I walked past the guards' office. I went to trailer number two and opened the door. It was total silence. Most of the people were asleep; the others were at work. I walked all the way to the end of the trailer where Cash was lying on the bottom bunk. He looked up at me in amazement that I was there. I smiled at him when he told me to sit down. I sat next to him and his face was as smooth as a *Dark and Lovely* commercial. He had on his wave cap, no shirt, and his gray sweat pants, as always. The print of his hard dick was just poking out staring straight at me. I leaned over and started to rub it. I massaged it up and down until it slid out of his boxers. I slid my hands into his sweats then started to massage it even more. He was long and fat. I could tell it was feeling good to him, although he was very nervous and kept looking back at the door to see if anyone was coming. He leaned back on the bed and I started to taste him. He was tasting good to me, then I glanced down at his feet. They were the ugliest toes I had ever seen! I never dreamed such a cute boy like Cash would have such ugly feet. That broke my concentration and I didn't want to carry on with him any longer.

I stood up and lied "Someone's coming." I would do anything to get out of that trailer and away from him. I told him that I would be back some other time.

The days were moving at a nice speed. Commissary came shortly after Fattman came in the trailer with a black eye. He was fighting some guy upstairs in the kitchen. I didn't know what that was about and really didn't want to know. All I knew was his eyes were shining. I was starting to get scared to work in the kitchen. I felt sorry for Fattman because he was cool with me. He didn't deserve that. Anyway, when commissary came I bought mostly socks and cosmetics because I needed some deodorant. Right away I noticed that a pair of my ankle socks were missing.

"Man you can't leave shit out around here!" That shit pissed me off. And, of course no one 'fessed up. Later on I found out James took them. Man, my own homie. That just goes to show you can't trust nobody.

I wasn't speaking to Country for the time being, and it seemed he was angry with me. One Saturday all of us were working on the front line. He was calling me all kinds of bitches and what not. Where did that come from? Every time I left the room he'd talk about me. It was pissing me off. I kept quiet, but then I thought about it, if he wanted to play that way then fine. I told everybody what he said to me and what he wanted to do. Everyone was shocked. I made it into a big issue; I even went to the gold badge guards and filed a report. Tony was nice, he made it clear that Country was not gonna lay a goddamn hand on me. Tony was acting as if he was my bodyguard and he made sure that Country was to stay at least fifty feet away from me. I had everyone on my side and Country was sent to the hole. Man I would hate to go there. It's a solitary cell where you sit, butt-ass naked, with no recreation whatsoever. So what, his ass deserved it.

We had a new addition to four trailer, a tall, light-skinned man name Kozeem. Koz for short. He was semi cute, and had a nice grade of hair. He noticed me as soon as he arrived. I introduced myself to him. He smiled. I smiled. As we talked, he filled me in on his long history, informing me that he'd been on lock down eight years! He also told me he could tell that I missed home. Man I guess anyone can see that by the sad expression on my face. He was in his late twenties, staring at me with his pretty slanted eyes. (by the way, he had some pretty feet.) He referred to me as Reggie-Reg or Reg Money. He was cool. He loved to draw and make greeting cards. He made a card for me to send home to my mother. That was sweet. I still had to pay him though. A pack of Newports would do the trick.

The eighth of July came. I was waiting anxiously for this day, my court day. After leaving work early, I went downstairs, took a shower, and put on a clean set of browns. I lie down on the bed and started watching *Three's Company* before falling asleep. I was awakened around ten o' clock by all the noise from the rest of the kitchen worker's getting off work. I wondered what had happened. Why wasn't I called for court? I fell into another state of depression. I phoned my mom because, again, she had taken off work and sat in the courtroom all day. She informed me that my judge was working on a rape case and that my probation officer was on vacation. Then she told me she called my probation officer and left a message on her machine stating that she was gonna "punch her in her head if shit don't get right!" I couldn't believe it. My mother just threatened the probation officer! Now I was certain I would never leave this place.

The next week they called James and me for court by surprise. Finally! We got dressed. Maybe today was the day I was gonna get to go home. I prayed, I prayed, and I prayed. (Again, Mary called my mother and told her that I had court, so she took off from work and met me just in time at the courthouse in Media, PA).

We started out first in outtake, where we had to wait for a total of three hours. It was cool. I waited there with James and a couple of other people I knew from the jail. I was sitting there laughing and joking with James when I turned my head and "Oh God!" There he was in his boxers, Mike-Mike. He was coming from the hole, so he didn't have on any clothes. This was the first time I'd ever laid eyes on him. He was the cutest boy I had ever seen: brown skin, pretty face, nice juicy full lips, curly black hair, and a nice muscular body. I smiled at him as he slipped his pants on. He was too cute for himself. He walked over to the holding cell where we were sitting—I just sat and stared at that one curl lying in the middle of his forehead.

"Wassup?" he said to James. They already knew one another, but he spoke to me as well. He had a tattoo on his right arm that read 'Mike $56.' Damn he looked good. He started to eat a big bag of Nachos. He shook all of our hands, then gave the bag to James to pass around. His smile was out of this world. I wondered why I had never seen this boy; where did he come from; what block was he on? He told us he'd been in the hole for throwing hot water on someone. Mike-Mike was crazy like that. Today was his sentencing day also. I couldn't believe my luck when I was handcuffed to Mike-Mike. We walked to the van. I gazed up at the sky, staring at all the different shaped clouds. They were so pretty. I knew I was going home. As we loaded up in the van I glanced over at James and wondered if he was ready for what the judge had in store for him. The sheriff turned the radio on. Brian's *Anytime* was playing and we all started to sing along. On the way, I prayed. As we approached the courthouse I could see where my mother's car was parked. She was sitting inside it reading the newspaper. We pulled into the garage where the waiting sheriffs accompanied us to our cells.

Since Mike-Mike and I were handcuffed together, we were assigned to the same holding cell, which had nothing but a cement bench and a toilet connected to a sink. Maybe we were meant for each other, I thought. It was just us two. Apparently he was from A-block. But how I never saw him before I couldn't say. As we talked, he took his shirt off and started to do some push-ups, then we played cards. For lunch they brought bologna. I hate bologna. James and I were hollering from cell to cell, cracking jokes. I gave my food to Mike-Mike. He offered me the rest of his juice, but I turned it down.

About ten minutes after Mike-Mike went to see the judge he returned, sat down, and stared straight ahead.

"What happened?" I asked quietly.

"I don't want to talk about it," he said, his eyes watering up. He put his hands over his face. He got up to put some water on his face and I stood up to the bars. I just wanted to go up to him and put my arm around him, but I didn't. It was about ninety-two degrees outside and one hundred degrees in here. There was total silence.

He turned around and said, "They gave me thirteen to twenty six years, Upstate."

My heart dropped. I wanted to reach out and take his head and put it on my shoulder. We both were quiet for the next half-hour, then he stood up a changed man. He started throwing bread around the cell and he wanted me to tie tissue paper around his head, legs and arms just so he could start rapping like he was Tupac.

Everyone had now seen the judge except for James and me. It was time to head back to the prison. I was hurt. I cried the entire trip back. The other inmates threw balls of tissue at me and called me faggot during the ride back. I was just paralyzed. I didn't care. I didn't even say bye to Mike-Mike. I just headed straight for the trailers. These muthafuckas were getting on my nerves and I didn't think I could take it anymore. Although it was summertime, the air-conditioned trailer was extremely cold and my feet were freezing. I attempted to lay in bed but I had to stop crying because my tears were cold running down my face. I got tired of people asking me what was wrong. I turned off my TV and just lay there. I thought about Mike-Mike. After that ride back in the van everyone now knew I had a crush on him, even him.

One day I was walking in the kitchen while he was in the chow hall eating. His head was bald. I guess he didn't want to go Upstate with pretty, curly hair.

The days were getting long and my heart couldn't stand the pain. I sang songs to myself and I prayed. The following Thursday, I finally went to court. I was sentenced to six to twenty three months in prison and one hundred and fifty-six hours of community service. Ain't that a bitch? I was mad as hell that I wasn't going home any time soon. James was sentenced to one hundred and fifty-four hours of community service upon completion of a drug rehabilitation program. Man was that a kick in the ass. Even James tried to calm my nerves by telling me that I was leaving before him, but it just did not work.

Since I wasn't leaving anytime soon, I decided to try and get a different job. Working the kitchen sucked. I didn't have any skills to be a barber, so that was out. I couldn't do any plumbing for the maintenance crew. I settled for moving to eight trailer, which was A.M. sanitation, meaning I had to clean the jail in the middle of the night. I guessed I could do that. It's not like I had anything else to do. Unfortunately, Nasir had been discharged the week before, so he was no longer in eight trailer. Radi was there, in and out, which was cool, but Jawan didn't want me to move in at all. He worked hard on the dirty looks he gave me. He tried to convince CO Brown that the trailer was a Muslim trailer and that it would be a sin to have me move in there. But, you know Brown, he wasn't havin' that. He told them he didn't care what kind of trailer it was, I was gonna be moving in there regardless. Since Jawan didn't get his way, he managed to get his own job changed. My bunk was the first one across from Kareem, who looked like a bum the way his hair was patted down on the top of his head. He had eyes like Garfield the cat, and he looked as if he'd been dragged out of the swamp. Kareem wanted me to move in just because I had a television and radio. He had a lot of girls writing him, I would guess because they liked his thug image. The bunk in front of me was Charles', who was a short Puerto Rican: nice, kind of cute, stocky. Although he was deaf, he was very cool. There wasn't really much that I could say to him, since I couldn't use sign language; Jawan always seemed to communicate with him just fine. While I was happy for Nasir being discharged, I sure wished he were there.

I moved in slowly. James had told me to hold his last pack of cigarettes, but I sold them for two shelves to go in my locker. When he found out I sold them, boy did he piss a bitch, and it was funny. I paid him back the next commissary day. I now had yellow shirt status, which gave me access to any block in the jail. I started my cleaning job that first night. It was easy. We only worked for an hour and a half. It was a breeze. I had to take trash out to the back and buff the chow hall floors. Now, I had never buffed a floor in my entire life, and that took some getting used to. During my rounds, I noticed that on some of the blocks the cells were tiny, only for two men. They were so small, you couldn't even do push-ups in them. I felt sorry for those guys.

At one point, I went over to E-block. "Ey Reg," I heard Teddy calling my name. "Come here," he yelled, his arms extended through the bars.

"I'm not coming to you," I said just to be smart.

Seeing as how I was now sentenced, I was able to get a printout of my charges. I went to the counselor who always seemed too busy. He resembled a chubby nerd from a television movie. My printout stated that I had good time and could be released on good behavior on August 28, 1998. But, if not then, I would get out on my minimum sentence, which was October 3, 1998.

"Well at least I will be out before the summer is over," I told James, who wasn't getting out until November.

Since I only worked two hours a day, I had a lot of time to kill. I listened to the radio a lot, especially Quiet Storm on 105.3 WDAS. I cried a lot, but didn't want anyone else to see me. I finally had a lock for my locker. I had to give Cash a whole pack of cigarettes for that lock. It didn't take long for it to go missing however. I went down to take a shower, came back, and it was gone. Not surprising. Shitty. But not surprising. I was sure it was that damn Kareem. He was the sneakiest person in the whole trailer. Of course he denied it.

The day Radi was being discharged was absolute commotion. He pulled sheets off of beds and made a lot of noise. Needless to say, I couldn't get any sleep before work.

I looked so cute in my yellow shirt, neatly pressed brown pants with elastic at the bottom, and orange and white Nikes. The guys on A-block loved it every time I came through. They loved to see my smile. One day my job was to scrub the walls down real good. But you know, the white man can always see spots, so I had to do the whole wall again. He threatened to fire me if I didn't do the job right. I was happy that the job only lasted for two hours. I couldn't wait to hurry back downstairs and listen to the *Quiet Storm*. When I got back to the trailer it just so happened that everyone was talking about gay people and, as soon as I walked in, all the attention was on me. They wanted to know all kinds of things, like who does who, how often do I have sex, and do I suck dick? Really, none of the questions that pertained to me were any of their business. I just turned my nose up at them and went to lie down.

One day Jawan had his boots stolen out of his locker. He was aware that I knew who had taken them, but I wasn't gonna fess up. He just sat there on the side of his bunk looking pitiful; for once he needed help. I told him I wasn't saying shit. But then I felt so bad. He was looking so helpless. The next day I went back and apologized. He was writing a letter to a girlfriend of his when I noticed a couple of misspelled words in his letter. So I sat down and helped him rewrite the letter.

James, Fattman, and Kozeem told me they missed me from trailer four. I must admit I missed them too. I missed the kitchen, especially the food part, and I even missed messing with Mary. It was tiresome living in eight trailer, where everyone was stealing from each other. I needed to decide if I wanted to give up my yellow shirt and go back to the kitchen. It didn't take long for me to make the right decision. This was such a noisy-ass trailer, no peace and quiet for nothing. That was it. I wanted to go back to four trailer and work in the kitchen. So I did.

Everyone was happy I was back. Jawan stated that he was happy to get that faggot out of the trailer. I even got the good bunk in four trailer, the one all the way at the end where Tony was. He had gotten his job changed to G-block runner so he moved out. I had a good view of the showers. My first night back, I saw Kozeem get in the shower. Man I wanted him. My eyes watered as I sat and watched that thang hang.

I was thrilled to be back in the kitchen. Mr. Perry lit a cigarette and he doesn't even smoke. His excuse was that since I was back he needed one. Right away I was tired and hot, but it was worth it. I did not want to go back to eight trailer for nothing. Even though I was working the kitchen, I started losing a lot of weight because I wasn't eating right. I missed home. I spoke to my mother on the phone and she informed me that she had made a meatloaf and mashed potatoes for dinner. I jokingly asked her to mail me a piece. Shit, I needed to eat something. During my breaks in the kitchen I would turn around and just stare at the wall with tears running down my face. Butler tried to console me, but it didn't help. I wanted to go home so bad. I started to get very annoyed at my job. Everyone wanted me to sing and dance, to keep them happy, but I wasn't happy. I was so fed up of being a slave. I wanted to die, but I just couldn't bring myself to do it. Mary fired me from the kitchen for insubordination. No matter what she said or how many things she told me to do, I would not do it. I knew my life in the trailers was over but I didn't care. I was going home in three weeks and couldn't wait.

My mother and cousin came to visit me. I walked up to them and gave them a hug. They both smiled at me and told me it was a nice night outside and they couldn't wait until I came home. We talked for our hour-long visit, then they left. Lord knows I wanted to leave with them.

Since I was fired I knew I'd have to move back on a block, but I never knew when that would happen. Mr. Perry was nice. He brought in some NyQuil to help me sleep. He wasn't supposed to bring in that type of stuff for the inmates, but he was cool. Whenever I needed help with something, he was there. It got boring just lying around everyday without working. Mostly I'd sit and talk to CO Brown or watch TV while everyone was at work. One day I decided to go outside during recreation. It seemed like one hundred degrees out there.

The counselor wanted to see me. When I got there my sentencing sheet was smack there in the middle of his desk. It was identical to the printout I had, but the August 28 date was crossed out. My eyes started to water as one tear rolled down my right cheek.

I wiped it away with the back of my hand and he looked up at me. I asked, "What happened?"

"You don't get good time on a second offense," he stated. I grabbed the paper and walked quietly back to my trailer. I could hear people calling my name, but I didn't answer. I just went to my bunk and lay down next to my radio where Natalie Cole's *I Got Love on My Mind* was playing. I grabbed my pillow tight and just sobbed. I cried, and I cried, and I cried. And then I cried some more. Later that day I sat at the table and had a long talk with Kozeem. We talked about a lot of things, which was good because now it was time for me to pack my shit.

James looked at my face and smiled saying, "I told you don't fuck with Mary." I ran down to eight trailer to tell Shyheed I was leaving, but he was high. He said he would take care of me no matter what. I needed peace of mind, which I wouldn't be getting, because I was taking my black ass back to E-block.

Back to E-block

I wasn't sad about moving. As a matter of fact, I didn't even care. It had just finished raining and the humidity was rising. I was very hot. I carried my TV, and Kareem had my bag and my box. We walked through chow hall. By then everyone that was eating knew that I had gotten fired from the kitchen and they were just staring at me. As always, I was the talk of the jail. This was no different than any other time. As soon as I got to E-block I called my mother. Everyone was on lock down when I got there, so I had total peace in the dayroom. Right away I started perspiring— sweat dripping down my face and from under my arms. When I arrived at the block, everyone was yelling and screaming from cell to cell. Even J-Rock was hollering like he was happy to have me back. He had moved from thirteen cell downstairs to four cell. The whole block was in an uproar. I was assigned to eighteen cell, on the top tier. I walked up the steps ignoring all the questions and name calling until I reached my cell. I looked at my bunk. Then it hit me. I couldn't believe I was back. It wasn't supposed to happen this way. I was back behind bars like a caged animal. Man, I thought I would never be back on this block again. I walked in the cell and one of my cellmates greeted me at the door.

"Wassup, I'm Speedy," he introduced himself. He already knew who I was from the mad reviews I was getting from the block. People were still yelling my name and I was yelling back. J-Rock and I joked and laughed for about fifteen minutes before I calmed down. Then Teddy started to holler at me asking more questions as to why I got fired from the kitchen, which was humiliating. Speedy was a chubby man, maybe in his late thirties or early forties. He was light-skinned with heavy facial hair. Rondell was my other cellmate. He was young, about in his early twenties, with brown skin and a medium build. He had a fever blister on his top lip that looked nasty as hell. There was also a white man that was lying on the bottom bunk, but he didn't say much. I glanced at him and he nodded his head. I nodded back.

Champs went down to pre-release so he could start his work-release program, so I didn't have anyone to look after me. Not even J-Rock because he had a whole new heap of friends.

Water from the rain came in through the windows and was all over the floor and our beds. I wiped my bed as Speedy grabbed for my television and set it aside so it wouldn't get wet. I glanced up at the ceiling and noticed the light bulb had a pink commissary paper covering it so the light wouldn't shine so bright. Speedy was working at the window, trying to keep the water from coming in. The humidity was very high and I couldn't wait to plug in my fan. Speedy had given me the bottom bunk, since I had a television. I tried to clean it and fix it up as much as I could. I put my sheets on the bed and hooked up the TV. The reception was great. The cell still looked empty so I put my quilt down on the floor to use as a rug.

The gates opened. That was a sound I'd hoped to never hear again. J-Rock came to my cell to talk. He had someone with him named Kevin. I always thought Kevin was cute. He was brown, with short wavy hair, and a sexy, cut body.

He had a tattoo on his bicep that read "Kev Money." He'd always walk the block with his brown pants on, boxers showing at the top, and a pair of blue New Balance sneakers. These Chester boys looked good.

After they left I lay back down and continued to watch *Martin*. I tried to take a nap but couldn't, due to all the noise from outside the cell. It was hot. The fan wasn't doing anything but blowing the hot air around. It was bad enough people kept coming in my cell asking me why I wasn't working in the kitchen anymore. By now I was missing the kitchen bad, missing the trailers, missing the air, and missing cracking jokes with James and Fattman. I missed being called the mother of the trailer. I was hungry. I wanted Shyheed. I was hoping he hadn't forgotten me. I felt alone. I was wondering if James was gonna bring me something to eat. He never did. I only had two soups left in my box until commissary.

I finally got up to use the phone. I called my mother at work, but she was off for the week so I figured I would give her a call the next day. I walked through the dayroom with a t-shirt, gym shorts, white socks and my shower shoes on. I had my hands tucked down in my shorts because I could feel all eyes were on me.

"Yo Reg!" Kevin hollered out, "What you got to eat?"

"Nothing," I answered.

"C'mon, I know you got something, kitchen boy. Got something to eat, to help a brotha out? I'm hungry and my belly is in my back. I see you gaining weight, so I know you eating good," he continued.

"I'll have to check," I told him. I happily walked back up to my cell and reached into my box. Both of the soups were gone. Somebody got them that fast.

Before I knew it, it was eleven o' clock, time to lock up. We had an older CO on the block named Presley. He was a big guy with slightly curly hair who would spit when he talked. He didn't play at all. He loved to write people up, which meant he loved sending people to the hole. When the bars closed and locked I just placed my head tightly down on my pillow. I couldn't believe I was back here. I was extremely hungry. About four o' clock in the morning Shyheed brought me a plate of eggs and grits from the kitchen. I jumped up to the bars and grabbed it like I was an animal. I couldn't thank him enough. He said that he would be back and not to worry. Soon they would have been calling for breakfast anyway, so I didn't go back to sleep, neither did Rondell. We stayed up and watched cartoons.

The next morning it was bright and sunny outside and I wished that I was home. I tried not to think about it. Today was Teddy's day to go to pre-release. I wasn't sad because I was still on the block with Kevin.

I went to see the counselor about going to pre-release and he told me I had to wait a week for the paperwork to go through. I waited and kept my cool.

Throughout the course of the week Speedy was starting to get on my nerves, talking about how he used to be a player and going with all these girls at one time. Bullshit. Rather than continuing to feel sorry for myself, and to get away from that crap, I decided to walk around the block and get familiar with the place again. I pranced around looking into people's cells thinking about what I could get into. I sold some of my Nyquil pills since I didn't have anything to eat. Other people needed them to go to sleep just as much as I did. I was getting a little comfortable again.

The weekend came and we were served those nasty ass bologna sandwiches on soggy bread. I sold mine for a soup. It was a hot, boring, and rainy weekend. The commissary came on Monday. My mother had sent some money, so I was able to rack up a lot of goods. I bought seven packs of cigarettes, in case I needed them for barter, a big bag of cheese popcorn, cheese curls, a bag of nachos, five Snicker bars, two Hershey bars, twelve soups, a pack of Twizzlers, a bag of Pizza Combos, a bag of Jolly Ranchers, two cans of Pepsi, a pair of socks, a washcloth, and a pack of peanut chews. I guess I was set for about a week. I placed my things in my box and covered it with the lid. It was dinnertime, so we requested to have our cell closed and locked before we left for the chow hall. There was a lady CO in the cage that particular day that opened everyone's cell before we all had a chance to come back from the chow hall. Sure enough, I walked from the hallway and up the stairs to my cell to find my box empty. I looked around and no one was in sight. I ran back down to the guards' cage and asked the CO why she had opened my cell. She argued with me until I requested to see the lieutenant. I had a little bit of pull around the jail now that I was a former worker in the trailers. She had no damn business opening the cells. I turned around and went back to my cell.

The bars closed and I yelled "If I don't get my shit back, I'm gonna have this whole block shaken down!" I wasn't playing. That meant all the drugs, cigarettes, and contraband would be confiscated and some people would be goin' to the hole. I just sat back on my bed and watched television. I was giving it a little time for someone to step forward. My mother sent me that money and I'd be damned if someone else benefited from it. I'm not goin' out like that. I continued to wait. About fifteen minutes later the ringleader of four cell came to my cell and asked me not to notify the gold badge and have the block shaken down. I looked at him as if he was trippin'. He told me to make a list of everything that was taken and he would see to it that everyone on the block chipped in to give me my things back. "Does this nigga take me for a fool?" I thought to myself. Clearly he took my shit. I knew it, but I just played along with his game. As long as I got my stuff back I wouldn't take it to center (center was where all the lieutenants' offices were). I sat back on the edge of my bunk, watched cartoons, and waited patiently.

Seven o' clock rolled around and the gates opened. J-Rock came to my cell with the majority of my things, minus two soups and a bag of cheese curls. I was cool with that. Hungry people needed to eat too. I took the food, placed it back in my gray box, and closed the lid.

The days were going by so slowly. I was hoping to go down to pre-release soon. I couldn't stand waiting. One day when I was in the chow hall I ran into Butler. He was down in pre-release and said it was real down there. It was almost like being free. He was happy and I was happy for him. He said he'd be waiting for me. And I was waiting to go.

The nights were warm. I sat in my cell, watched television, and joked around with Rondell and Speedy. We talked about what we were gonna do when we left this place and how we were gonna get our lives together. I was so hot I couldn't move. I was running out of t-shirts. I washed the same shirt everyday in the sink and hung it up to dry on our clothesline. My socks were dingy, so I didn't even bother to wear any. I walked out and stood on the top tier and placed my arms on the railings and stared down at the fella's playing cards and chess. I had always wanted to learn to play chess but never took the time. Now I had all the time in the world to do a lot of things: think, sleep, and catch up on my television shows. I glanced up at the ceiling where I could see the sky through an opening. I wished I were out there somewhere.

Monday morning was the same ol' same ol'. I skipped breakfast because they were serving that shit on a shingle again. I wasn't about to put that in my mouth. I lay there in bed with my face flat in the pillow and prayed silently. I rolled over and was watching TV when CO Presley told me I would be going to pre-release today. That was the best news I had heard all summer long.

I went to lunch where they were serving hamburgers. I needed one. I was hungry. But before I ate I had to go to outtake and get my picture taken for my ID badge for pre-release. I ran to outtake with happiness and smiled at the camera. I went back to the block to pack my things. I was so excited to be leaving. I took my pictures off the wall, folded my sheets and the little bit of clothes I owned. I let Speedy and Rondell watch my television until it was time for me to leave. Presley yelled out my name and the gate opened. I was ready to go. I unhooked my TV and told everyone goodbye. PEACE!

Pre-Release

I was so happy to finally carry my things to outtake. Although I wasn't going home, it was good to leave the building. I took off my brown shirt and kept my t-shirt on. While I was in outtake I had to transfer all of my things out of the gray box into a clear plastic bag. A couple of other people along with myself had to wait for the van to come get us. We all sat outside where it was hot as hell. The van arrived and I hopped in the front. In spite of the heat, I was happy to smell the fresh air. I rode with the window down, closed my eyes, and took a deep breath. I said a silent prayer, thanking God for getting me out of that jail.

We stopped in front of a long yellow brick building. I jumped out the van and went inside. I sat my stuff down and looked around at the vending machines and pay telephones. The guards weren't behind cages and it seemed much cleaner compared to the jail. We were taken to the other side of the building, which was the weekend side, to discuss the rules and regulations. Pre-release was divided into three different parts: work release, the weekend side, and pre-release, which was where I was assigned. We weren't allowed on either side unless we asked. The Lieutenant for pre-release was a young white woman. She was very beautiful and very nice. Her name was Lieutenant Blisseron. She was in her mid-twenties and had long, golden-blond hair and a smile that could light up any room. She talked for a while. With her were a couple of inmates who served as block reps. Tyriq was a petite, dark-skinned block rep, with short black wavy hair; Mark was chubby and brown, with a low haircut— he worked in the kitchen; and then there was Clarence, who took care of the laundry. He was an older guy with a broken foot. They all welcomed us to pre-release. After they talked for about 15 minutes I called my mom to let her know where I was. She told me she would be up there the next day. We were allowed ten dollars in quarters for the vending machines and to make phone calls, so she said she would bring me some.

I felt like a fish out of water. The place was empty because everyone was out on a work assignment. I walked round. There were about thirty-six cubicles with one set of bunk beds in each. These bunk beds were made with real springs and I could not wait to lie down on one. I was in cube 34, all the way in the back. The person I was sharing the cube with didn't get along with me and I didn't get along with him. Actually, I couldn't stand him.

Later that day I saw Arnold, Butler, and Champs. They were all happy to see me. The boy in my cube had to move out because he was having trouble with other people back there besides me. So there I was, all alone in my cube. I placed my television on two crates. About three times a day, everyone had to be in their cubes for count. I knew most of the COs. Some of them were the same ones that worked in the jail. They were surprised and very happy to see me down there.

Champs gave me a dollar and Arnold gave me some change for something from the vending machines to get through that first day. Arnold also cut my hair because I had a visitor coming the next day.

My first night on pre-release I didn't get any sleep. My throat was killing me and I was excited about seeing my mother the next day. Arnold came in my cube and sat on the side of my bed. It felt weird to have company after hours I thought to myself. He looked at me. It was dark, so he couldn't tell if I was looking at him or not. All day he kept telling me that he had something to ask me. I guessed he was going to finally ask it.

"Are you gay?" he asked. He certainly didn't beat around the bush.

"Why?" I asked.

"Well, can I have a kiss?" I was shocked, but I'd had a feeling he liked me. Arnold was a slim guy, light-skinned, with a nappy bush. He had a gap between his two front teeth.

"No!" was my reply. "What made you ask me for a kiss?" I asked. Then he went on to say that I had pretty lips and what not. The same story I'd heard from the rest of these hormonal men. I asked him if he was gonna cut my hair for free the next time that I needed a haircut.

Then he stood up in front of me with his hard dick that was stretching through his sweat pants and said, "you tell me," and walked away. I lay back down considering what had just happened. I wasn't sure what he really wanted from me.

A half an hour later, Terrance came to my cube, who I didn't find to be overly attractive.

"Do you have any cigarettes?" he asked.

"No, I don't smoke," I replied.

He turned and walked away. Then he came back and sat on the side of the bed, the same place where Arnold had been sitting.

"What?" I asked.

"Come over to the shower, I have to show you something," he quietly whispered.

"I don't feel like it," I said. "Show me right here."

"I can't, because you need more light."

"All right, I'll be there in three minutes," I lied. He left and headed towards the showers. A few minutes later he came back.

"What happened?"

"I don't feel like it," I told him. "Oh, all right," I said.

He left again, and this time I followed a few minutes later. It was semi dark and everyone was asleep. The back of the building was dark; the only light that was shining was coming from the guards' office. I walked to the bathroom, back toward the showers, and there he was, ass-naked in one of the showers, stroking his dick, up and down. I looked at him, then glanced at myself in the mirror.

"What you think?" he asked. "You like it?"

"Not really," I responded.

"It's big ain't it?" He said.

I turned around and walked back out of the bathroom and back to my bunk. He followed me.

"Let's do it," he said with a smile on his face.

Who the fuck do these niggas think I am, I thought? I lay down on the bed.

"So do you want to?" He asked. His straining dick told me he was at my mercy.

"No," I answered him. Then he pulled out his dick and started to stroke it again. I laughed.

"You know you want to," he said.

"No, the fuck I don't!" I responded. He looked at me, stroking harder. Before I could say anything else, semen was all over the floor, dripping from his hands.

"You betta clean that shit up," I told him, jumping up from the bed. I unrolled the toilet paper and passed it to him as he wiped every bit of that nasty ass cum up off the floor. I lay back down and he left, putting the toilet paper in the trash can.

It was morning and Ron woke me up. He was on his way to work. He had on a yellow Polo shirt and a pair of black jeans. He was admiring my sneakers and said he wanted to buy them. I told him I wasn't selling them, and besides, I needed something to do community service in.

Mark and Tyriq were running around cleaning up the building so they could watch cartoons when were finished. They were very close. They were from the same town in Chester, and they acted as if they were partners in crime. I told the community service supervisor, John, that I couldn't go out with him that day because I was getting a visit from my mom. He was cool with that.

Everyone that had somewhere to go that day, left. A couple of us stayed behind, including Mark, Tyriq, Arnold, and a couple of others. Arnold gave my hair a shape-up and Tyriq watched. I sat there on top of the crates and listened to them talk about girls and what they were going to do when they went home. When Arnold finished, I looked in the mirror. My hair was sharp. I couldn't wait to wash it so I could be ready for my visit. Tyriq stared at me while I was admiring myself in the mirror. I placed the mirror on the side of the sink and he walked over to me. He was very short; the top of his head barely reached my neck. He put his dark lips near my ear.

"As long as I'm here, you don't have to worry about nuffin," he said. Then he handed me two dollars in quarters to use the phone. I was impressed. His technique was very straight and to the point. He was so small and so cute. He reminded me of my cousin. I headed to the shower. On weekdays, the visits for pre-release were held in our dayroom and on weekends they were up at the jail.

My mother came at the exact time she said she would. I walked into the dayroom after being searched, and there she was, sitting with a rag covering her mouth. She said she had been to the dentist where they'd been operating on her teeth and she was in a great deal of pain. I felt bad that she had to come all the way out here in such a predicament. We hugged and then talked for a while. She gave me a roll of quarters and explained how things were back home. She was still struggling to pay her mortgage and didn't think she'd be able to keep it up. I sure didn't want to be goin' through the things she was going through, on top of dealing with me in here, but what could I do?

When the visit was over, I went back to my bunk to take a nap. I slept 'til about five o'clock, when it was time to eat. Pre-release was so much better than being up at the jail. We could eat in the dayroom with our shorts on, rather than having to put on our browns. (In pre-release we wore "tans.")

The next day I had community service. I had on my white Nikes, a pair of tans, and a bright white tee-shirt. I was clean. It was hot as hell outside. That day our community service instructor was a white man named Tom. He was an older guy, probably in his early 60's. He made it clear that he didn't like homosexuals. I think he didn't like blacks either but that was a different story. Just by the way we met the first time I could tell that he couldn't stand me.

I was happy to be outside again: riding through the streets, seeing the cars, and the people. Just the outside life made me happy, 'til I had to start working. We had to chop down some big ass trees and I wasn't used to manual labor.

"You fuckin' faggot!" Tom yelled out to me.

I turned around and he looked at me as he mumbled under his breath. I was the biggest dummy out there in his eyes. I didn't say anything. I was scared to even touch the trees because I could have been hurt. I just looked at Tom with sweat rolling down my face. My t-shirt wasn't white anymore, and my Nikes were extremely dirty. My allergies started to get the better of me. I was having sneezing fits, my eyes were watering, and I could feel myself getting lightheaded. Tom told me to sit down. He said he wasn't gonna give me credit for that day. I was so tired. I had never done anything like that before in my life.

When we got back I wanted to sleep. I had to be up at seven o' clock the next morning. I wanted to talk to someone about Tom's attitude, but no one would listen.

The weekend couldn't come fast enough. I slept the whole weekend. I was up Saturday night hanging around with Mark and Tyriq. We watched videos and played cards. I was very amused when Lauryn Hill's *Doo Wop* video came on. Arnold came and sat next to me. He took off his shoes and leaned back. I wanted to tell him to get the hell out of my cube, but I didn't. I just took off to Mark's cube. Mark, Tyriq, and Chappell were there, smoking Blacks and Mild. When I went back to my cube Arnold was gone. A few minutes later, Tyriq came in. He had two cheese steaks in his hand. He put them on the side of my bed.

"Here baby," he said. I was kind of hungry but I wasn't starving. He left the cube and I started to eat. When he came back about a half an hour later he said I turned him on. He had on sweat pants and his dick was hard. I touched it through his pants and knew it was a cute size for his body. He pulled it out, grabbed my head, and moved it towards it. I snatched my head back. I felt his dick, smiled, and put it back in his pants. He rolled his eyes at me and darted out of the cube.

The weekend was over and it was Monday. Back to community service. It was eight o'clock in the morning and I wasn't ready. Today was John's day. What a relief, he didn't give me nearly the hassle that Tom did. I cleaned my sneakers and put on another white t-shirt and was out the door.

The morning started off great. We had ham and cheese sandwiches for lunch and fruit punch juice to drink. We went to the woods in far out Delaware County, where we had to clean out the swamp. The process was chopping down trees and digging items out of the creek. It was hot. I never knew my whole body could sweat all at once. I tried so hard to find shade. There was none. I was having a hard time standing up. I pulled off my shirt and found these little white puss balls all over my stomach and chest. I wanted to go home so bad. I thought about running. But then I figured that's more time and I wasn't about to sit in jail longer than I had to. Finally we headed back.

I prayed to the Lord to see better days. I went straight for the showers. I didn't know what was on my stomach, but when I looked down later that day they were gone. I needed something for my allergies.

The lieutenant moved my cube from the back to the front of the building where her office was. I didn't know why, and she wouldn't say. I was now in the front with all the noise and all the bright lights. It started to rain. Everyone was out there using the phones. The lights were bright. I couldn't sleep. I needed to use the phone bad. I needed to talk to someone. I slipped over to the weekenders' side to use the phone, just real fast. I didn't even have time to dial the number before I was caught. The CO didn't even give me a break.

"Pack your shit," was all he said. I went to my cube and nervously packed my stuff. I thought I was cool with both of the COs in there, but I guessed wrong. The other CO insisted that I be given a break, but it wasn't flying. Tyriq was mopping the floor and looking up at me telling me that I never listen. The constables came through the door and placed the handcuffs on me.

"Get that faggot outta here!" someone yelled from the back. I walked through the door, hopped in the back of the van and rode back up to the jail.

F-Block

It was kind of damp outside from the rain. I had on my shower shoes and my hands were placed in cuffs to the front of me. How I wished I could turn back time. He could have given me another chance. Back through the doors and up the steps to intake. Here I go again, I thought to myself. I went back into the holding cell.

I called my mother and told her what had happened. She was just as upset as I was. I guess it didn't matter too much. I was getting out in thirty days.

The new people coming in to F-block were dirty and disgusting: drug dealers, bums, and prostitutes. I took off my tans and put on a brown suit that read 'Intake' in big, bright, letters. The COs were laughing at me. I knew what I did was dumb, but everyone makes mistakes. I just sat in the holding cell and talked on the phone. I talked to my brothers, my grandmom, and my cousins. About three o' clock in the morning, they were ready to take us upstairs. By that time I was so tired. I just wanted to go to sleep. We headed upstairs to our holding cell where I went in and fell right to sleep.

I woke up the next morning and had to go to a hearing to see if I was guilty of talking on the phone on the weekenders' side. Of course, I was guilty.

I asked the counselor if she could put me on F-block because I knew if I was to go back to E-block I would be too embarrassed. I walked back upstairs to the holding cell to lie down. I stared at the ceiling. I thought about home and how it seemed like I was never gonna get there. I wouldn't be able to go back to pre-release for thirty days, which was when I was going home. I planned to just chill out on F-block until my thirty days were up. The holding cell was so quiet at this time. No one was talking. They were either deep in thought or deep in sleep. I fell asleep.

Before I knew it three days had passed, I was still in intake, and I hadn't taken a shower. My socks were dirty, my underarms smelled like onions, and my head was flaking up. I needed to change my underwear but I couldn't because my things where still down in pre-release. About seven o' clock a.m. the gates opened. It was time to be taken to the block. I took off the brown intake suit and put on a regular brown suit. My shirt was too small and my pants were too long; they were dragging under my slippers, which was not comfortable.

"Where's my stuff?" I asked the CO. He said it was still down the hill.

He opened the door to the block; we walked through E-block and on to F-block. When we reached F-block I walked past the guards' cage, onto the block, and up the steps toward my new quarters, twenty cell.

"You comin' in here?" asked Ameen. He was standing behind the bars of twenty cell. Ameen was tall, thin, and brown-skinned.

"Yeah," I answered. "With my TV." Next to Ameen was Bryan, a short, stocky, light-skinned guy. Bryan and I had been in elementary school together. In the back was Habib. He was Muslim, real quiet, and as far as I could tell, dumb.

They seemed very relieved that they could watch TV right there in the cell.

"You like my cousin, don't you?" hollered out Mike-Mike's cousin Greg, who was in fifteen cell. I didn't answer.

I just looked at him. The gates opened and I picked up my box and walked into the dirty cell. There was a puddle of water in the middle of the floor and I looked up to see that the light bulb was broken. Toilet tissue covered the toilet seat. I put my box on top of the water in the middle of the floor, sat on it and stared out the window. I continued to sit there, waiting for my other things to arrive. Finally I got up and ran to the guards' cage.

"Did you call for my stuff yet?" I asked.

"Yeah, they said that they would bring it up after count," he said. I was pissed. I was stinking and these damn pants did not fit right. Everyone kept asking about me getting shipped back, and I was tired of talking. I sat on a big brown wooden box outside of the guards' cage until it was time for lockdown.

Four hours later, it was eleven o'clock. Time for lockdown. The CO blew the whistle.

"Lock up!" he yelled. I continued to sit there. He looked at me.

"Time for lockdown, homie," he said, gently.

"No, I'm not locking up without my stuff," I said. After everything was secured, he gave me a pass to the Center. I hopped down off the box and walked through the chow hall where Kareem was buffing the floors. He had a smile on his face.

"What the fuck you smiling for?" I asked him, and he started to laugh. I proceeded to Center where all the guards were standing around talking like they didn't have a care in the world. I noticed my bag over in the corner and walked towards it. I checked it to see if everything was there.

I walked back to F-Block. The CO was nice enough to let me take a shower before I locked down. It was so nice to have the hot water touch my face and body. I washed my hair and my armpits. I scrubbed myself like I had never scrubbed before. When I got back to the cell I hooked up my TV, but the reception was a mess. I was so hungry; we had egg salad for dinner and I can't stand the smell or the sight of it. I was starving. I had a pop tart in my box, which I shared with the block rep, Hasaan. Hasaan was a silly, young, skinny brother. He loved to play. He had a hairy chest and sort of looked like Garfield the cat. I made my bed on the bottom bunk. Habib was nice enough to give me his bunk since I had a TV.

I slept good. It was Saturday when I woke up. I grabbed my envelope from under my mattress and crossed off another day on the calendar. In the envelope were letters from loved ones, and some pages of my thoughts. I was considering writing a book called *Delaware County Prison*, but wasn't sure it would sell. We had to eat our lunches on the block due to the visitors in the chow hall. They served "turkey ham" on trays. I didn't eat that shit. There is no such thing. Turkey is turkey and ham is ham! Once again, I starved.

We played cards throughout that day. At one point I was approached by a gang of Muslims. About nine of them crowded my cell, the ringleader came forward.

"I understand that you demanded something from a Muslim brother?" he said.

"What are you talking about?"

"You demanded the bottom bunk from brother Habib," he continued.

"I didn't demand anything." Then Habib walked in.

"Did he demand the bottom bunk from you?" they asked him.

"No," he said. They were just as confused as I was. All of this for nothing. Was it worth going to the hole, I thought to myself? That's why I don't like being around Muslims; they don't have any respect or consideration for non-Muslims.

The days went on and I marked them off my calendar. The people in my cell were starting to get to me. I needed peace and quiet, and they were making too much noise. What's worse, they didn't take showers and the smell was getting to me. Ameen said his skin was sensitive and he didn't want the hard water to hit it. Bryan only took a shower once a week. They had the nerve to argue with me about what I wanted to watch. Bryan threatened to break my TV if he couldn't watch the football game. Can you get any more ignorant? I hated it here. On Sundays I'd lay in the bed holding my pillow tight, crying, and listen to WDAS – especially the oldies after 7:00 p.m. Mostly I'd stay in my cell. Sometimes I'd use the phone, or spend time talking to the CO, if he was cool. Or I would play around with Curls, so nicknamed because of the curls on his head. He was skinny and missing a tooth from the front of his mouth. He called me Tiffany! He stole some food out of Ameen's box because he thought it was mine. Ameen was gonna whip his ass. He told Ameen he thought it was the faggot's. Every now and then I would get a visit from Tysean. He was from Chester and he, too, was Muslim. He was also scary. He'd come into my cell looking for juice, although I never had any. He asked to see the pictures of my cousins that were stuck to my wall with toothpaste.

He thought he was the king of F-block because he was big and knew that most people were afraid of him. He seemed very bold about what he wanted. He'd stand by us and rub himself while smiling at me, Ameen, and Bryan. They thought it would just be a matter of time before he tried to rape me.

All was not well. I hated it here. I walked out of my cell to see a fight; some white guy was beaten because he was in there for beating up his mother. My mother explained to me that when someone goes to jail for rape, child molestation, or for hitting their mothers, that's what happens.

I had to wash my t-shirts and socks by hand in the sink and hang them on the side of the bunk to dry. I didn't like walking around without any underwear on. I needed some new ones. My mother sent me a twenty-five dollar money order that wouldn't be processed 'til the next week.

All I could think about was food. I kept thinking about the store at the corner of my grandmother's block where I used to get a three-piece chicken order and fries with salt, pepper, and a little bit of ketchup. I dreamed of the day when I could get some. Knowing I was going home in two weeks was making me feel happy inside. I couldn't wait.

Habib beat his case, which was a rape case. He had been locked up for eight months. He was being discharged tonight. He came back from court extremely happy. I lay in my bed listening to the radio. Around six o' clock the gates opened. Habib walked out the cell and didn't look back.

Later that day we got a new cellmate, Marcus. He was young, attractive, and very energetic. He was from Chester as well, and he and Ameen got along fine. He was so rowdy and loved to make noise; the worst partner for Ameen to have. They sat up every night playing cards and being wild 'til about five or six in the morning. I hated it. I couldn't get any rest. Marcus was starting to test my patience. He'd wet the end of a towel and smack me with it. My legs had welts and scars on them, but he wouldn't stop. I wanted to fight Marcus so bad, but I knew if I was to fight I would go to the hole and I didn't want to be there, no way.

One day Tysean tapped me on my ass and the other inmates laughed. I didn't think it was funny. I took my television out of the window and sat it on my box next to my bed so only I could watch it. Poor Hasaan would come and try to make peace between us and persuade me to put it back in the window. I wasn't a drinker, but I found myself wanting a drink bad. Maybe I could get a 13-day binger going so I wouldn't feel anything until they told me I could walk.

A few days later, I was browsing around the block, shopping for a new cell. If I stayed in that cell any longer I was gonna lose it. I moved into sixteen cell with a few older guys, definitely a more relaxed crowd. I loved it. I could sleep peacefully and I didn't have to argue about my own TV. My new cellmates just mostly played cards. Marcus,

Bryan, and Ameen were very upset to see my television go. The first afternoon in my new cell I took a nice peaceful nap, watched *Ducktales*, and then fell asleep until it was time for chow.

The weekend was approaching. I was going home in seven days! My mother was happy and so was I. I was walking around like I owned the joint. Couldn't nobody tell me a thing. I was being a true man: singing rap songs and grabbing my crotch with bass in my voice. I was singing the words to Silk the Shocker's *It Ain't My Fault,* and people finally saw me for the man I really was. They didn't know I had it in me. Shoot, I didn't either. I was glad to be going home. I wanted to see my friends and my family. I was having a good time in sixteen cell. I just loved not having to argue all the time. I loved sleeping in late. I could jut relax without any bother from anyone.

The boys from H-block came to cut our hair. Since I knew them, I had a lot of pull and could get my haircut first and for free. He shaped up my eyebrows and my mustache. I was looking good. He passed me the mirror so I could admire my haircut. I loved it. People in the dayroom were astonished at my new do. I ran into Curls.

"Hey Cutie, nice haircut!" he said.

I walked into my cell and looked in the mirror once again. I liked it, but it needed a wash. I gathered all my cosmetics and took off my pants to head to the shower. I walked from my bed to the door with my t-shirt and boxers on, but before I could get to the door Tysean came in. I was alone in the cell. I stood next to the door and he walked around me and sat on my bed. I wanted him to get up but I knew, if I asked him he wouldn't.

"What are you about to do?" he asked.

"About to get in the shower," I responded nervously. One of my cellmates walked in, grabbed a deck of cards, and walked out.

"Come here," he said. My other cellmate came in, sat down on the side of the bunk, and started watching television. Tysean then called me over to him again. He started looking at my pictures on the wall.

"If you seen them once, you've seen them a thousand times," I said. I walked over to the bed and sat down beside him. I pulled my shirt down then closed my legs together. He grabbed my arm.

"Stop, get off me," I said.

"Come here, you are my bitch!" he said as his grip got tighter. He yanked on my boxers.

"Get off me please," I said in a calm voice but that didn't relieve his grip. My cellmate continued to watch television, completely without care about what was going on. Tysean pulled on my boxers again. I grabbed his wrist. I could feel how strong he was through the veins in his arm. He pulled harder. I could feel the thickness of his arms as he tugged my underwear; each time he tugged I could hear them rip. He then put his fist up under the right leg of my boxers then tugged harder. It was total silence except for the TV showing a toothpaste commercial. He tore my boxers completely off of me. I tried not to move. I knew if I moved he'd hit me and with one punch he would dislocate my entire face. I was already exposed. He sat there and looked at me. I slowly got up as I could feel a tear slither down my cheek. He still had a torn piece of my underwear in his hand. I pulled my t-shirt down to cover my rear. He grabbed my arm and pulled me back down on the bed with him. My dumb-ass cellmate continued to watch TV. I could feel a tear running down my cheek.

"Cry, yeah, that's what I wanna see," he said, in a monstrous voice. I signaled my cellmate to get the CO, but he didn't get up. I wished this wasn't happening. Tysean's grip loosened. He walked over to the doorway. I sat there with nothing on but an undershirt.

"Will you let me out?" I asked. Of course his answer was no.

I said a silent prayer, asking God to make Tysean stop. Tysean stood in the doorway for about twenty minutes just staring at me.

"Clean ya' self up," he said as he walked away smiling at the world.

I yanked the plug from my TV out of the wall. My cellmate looked up at me. I was fucking furious.

"How the fuck could you sit there and watch that happen to me?" I yelled.

He just sat there with a confused look on his face. I put my pants on and ran down to the guards' cage. I explained to the CO what had happened. He laughed and then told me it was time for lock up. I called my mom.

The rest of the night I didn't say anything to anybody. They laughed at the whole incident, but I didn't find anything funny.

It got out on the block about what Tysean tried to do to me, but he denied everything. Monday morning came and CO Presley was on duty. I was in a deep sleep, dreaming about home; I could hear the loud roar of the gate opening but I wasn't fully awake. I felt someone shaking me.

"Reg, wake up," I slowly opened my eyes to Marcus.

"Tysean is on his way in here to fuck you up," he said, quickly leaving the cell.

I jumped up, rushing to put my brown pants on, and ran downstairs and sat next to Presley on the bench. Tysean threw a bucket of hot water, missing me, but it hit Presley.

"Pack ya' shit, cause you goin' to the hole!" Presley yelled. "You tried to rape this boy the other night?" Presley continued.

I ran behind the other CO as Presley called back up on his walkie-talkie. The lieutenant came and escorted Tysean to the hole. They also wanted to put me in protective custody. Hell no, I can't go there, I thought to myself. Then it was decided that I should go to B-block.

"Why do I have to move, I didn't do anything?" I asked.

They told me that one of Tysean's friends was bound to hurt me if I stayed on F-Block. I didn't ask any more questions. I went back upstairs to my cell. Everyone was standing around wondering what was goin' on. Marcus came into my cell.

"Thanks, man," I said, realizing that if it wasn't for him who knows what might have happened. He smiled at me.

"C'mon now, let's go," Presley yelled up the stairs. I packed my stuff. I took everything that belonged to me and headed to B-block. Moving was worth it.

B-block

On the way out I had to stop at the nurse. She checked me out for bruises or marks of any kind. The lieutenant came in to the nurse's office to see if I was ok. He was cool. He asked me questions about what happened and stayed and talked with me until it was time for me to leave. The other COs in the hallway were having a discussion about me going to J-block.

"No, he's going to B-block," he said cheerfully. The first thing that came to my mind was B-block, two men cells. I didn't think I could take it.

I was mad, scared, and really nervous about this whole thing. I kicked my box through the dayroom of B-block and walked onto the block. I was getting looks from everyone. It gave me the creeps. I stared back. I turned to ask the CO what cell was I in. He told me nine cell.

"You're in a cell with a faggot!" someone yelled out.

I stood by the guards' cage for about twenty minutes. A gate separated B-block and protective custody. The block seemed way bigger than E- and F-block. Everyone walking past me stared at my TV and me.

Bullet walked by, Mike-Mike's cousin. He was tall, about six feet, and cute, brown-skinned with chinky eyes. He kept his hair low with a few waves flowing throughout.

"Wassup," he said, smiling. He was charming, real sweet, and had a boyfriend on A-block named Tracy. They shared the same cell. Man, I was in love with his eyes. B-block and A-block were right next to each other. Inmates from A-block had to walk through B-block to get anywhere in the jail.

A new guy walked up.

"Hi, my name is Lamont and I don't want to offend you but I'm gay," he said in a very deep voice. He was my new cellmate. I just stared at him for a moment.

"Well. I am too."

"Are you?" he asked, and his face lit up with relief. He took my box, I picked up my TV, and we both walked over to the cell. I walked in and did my usual look around. It was very small. It had one set of metal bunk beds and a toilet with a sink attached to it. Lamont had all his cosmetics in the windowsill. He gave me the bottom bunk and he took the top. Then Tracy entered. Lamont introduced us. He seemed very nice. I checked him out from head to toe. He was dark-skinned with black hair and a ponytail, probably in his early 30's. I could tell he and Lamont were real close. Turns out they were both from Chester. Lamont and Tracy talked for about five minutes as I settled in. I felt cozy. Even though the cell was extremely small, I made it homey. Tracy and I started to discuss boys. He informed me about the boys in the block. Before I could say anything he told me about Bullet and how they were an item, so he was off limits. Then he pointed straight across from me to six cell, telling me about the boy he'd had a crush on, and how he wasn't gay and didn't like homos. Anthony, that was his name. He was about 5 feet 8 inches, brown-skinned with curly hair, a pretty boy. Tracy explained how he wanted him since he first saw him.

"He's cute," I said. But he wasn't really my type. Little did Tracy know, I still had my eyes on Bullet.

I continued to make up my bed. Lamont was telling me about how he came to jail and how the people in B-block treated him like trash. Lamont and Tracy were extremely feminine. They referred to one another as girlfriends. After Tracy left, Lamont and I talked for hours. It was nice to have someone to talk to, someone who understood what I was all about. He told me that in a matter of time the guys on the block would start to approach me and boy was he right.

All that day Lamont just showed me around and introduced me to his boyfriend, David. Lamont was in love with David. David was a huge man who didn't take any shit from no one. He was cool. I was glad to be on his side. I only had four days left and was marking them off. Lamont and I talked and watched television all night long. The cell was private and comfortable. Lamont was more like a friend or even a sister than a cellmate. It was nice. Tracey came on the block periodically. Although he had Bullet, his eyes were still on Anthony. Anthony made it clear that he didn't go that way. He was a very respectful person. He'd come to our cell and talk to Lamont and me. He even would eat with us sometimes. He was real cool. It was out that I was from West Philly and he was too, from the same neighborhood.

But he was in his mid-20's and I was nineteen so we didn't know each other. But he knew my cousins.

I was feeling pretty good. I was leaving in a couple of days and couldn't wait to get home. I told my mom I had moved to B-block and she was happy that I had gotten away from Tysean.

That first night numerous people came to me telling me that Bullet wanted to see me at the door that separates A-block from B-block. I didn't pay any attention to the first two, but when the third person came and told me the same thing I headed that way.

"What are you doing?" he asked, smiling.

"Nothing, I'm bored," I said.

"Do you want me to come spend the night with you?" he asked.

I laughed. This guy is trying to get with me behind Tracy's back.

"Don't you already have someone to spend the night with?"

"Yeah, but that's just a some time thing," he explained. I laughed at him and walked back to my cell. Even though I had a crush on him I wasn't about to get involved in that bullshit.

There were some cuties in PC (protective custody). I had my eye on one boy named A.J. He was only 17 and man was he fine. He was brown-skinned with a low haircut with waves, dreamy eyes, and was pigeon-toed. He was sexy as hell. He'd always wear a V-neck undershirt where you could see his chest hairs, gray sweatpants, and a pair of white New Balance sneakers. He drove me crazy. I discussed him with Lamont and Tracy, trying to figure out what to do. I went in my cell and wrote him a nice love letter. I told him I was checkin' him out and how I thought he was mad cute. I nervously slipped it under the gate. He took the letter into his cell and read it. I waited anxiously for a response. He told me that he would write me a letter after dinner.

After dinner he slipped a letter under the gate and I grabbed it. B-block and PC would alternate lock down times, so when I was in, he was out, and vice versa. The letter was real satisfying. He said he felt the same way about me, that I was very attractive, and he wouldn't mind being my boyfriend. All day and all night I thought of A.J. He was a vision, the man of my dreams. He called himself Daddy Thug and called me Baby Thug. I loved it. Everyday we'd write letters back and forth to each other, sometimes five letters in one day. Lamont and I would just smile at each other when we read the letters. I was in love and Lamont was in love, although he would get dick on a normal basis. He'd sneak into twenty-one cell and put a sheet over the bars. Lamont would come back to the cell walking a little strange. I could tell that whatever happened, it hurt Lamont bad, but he loved it.

"Oooooh girl, he dicked me down," Lamont would say to me when he returned to the cell. I laughed. "I can't even sit straight," he'd go on. I didn't know how he could take it everyday. He'd keep himself clean by squeezing water from the baby oil bottle up his anus. I didn't think I could handle that; having sex without a condom behind these walls was bad enough, but all the cum Lamont had stuffed up his butt was more than I could take.

I would go nuts waiting for letters from A.J. I'd walk up the steps to the top tier and go over to the gate and chat with him. A.J. demanded a lot from me, mostly cigarettes and food. He always wanted me to go around asking people on the block for cigarettes. I hated that. But he was my man and I stood by him no matter what. Being the center of attention was good for me. Walking back from chow, swinging my plastic cup in my hand, made me feel like a natural woman.

Two more days and I was leaving. While we were waiting for the gate to our cell to open I noticed this strange guy staring at me. I tried my best not to keep looking at him but I just couldn't help it. He made sure I noticed that he was noticing me.

"Why does he keep looking at you?" asked Lamont. "You know he's crazy," he added. The guy then stood up and walked over to me.

"I don't want you to take this the wrong way or anything, but I think you have some attractive lips," he said. "I remember when you used to be a yellow shirt and came over to the block. I said to myself that you were very attractive and I'm not even gay," he continued.

"Thank you," I said, not knowing what else to say. My body was screaming for some type of affection. I needed someone to kiss these lips bad. I smiled at him and Lamont smiled at me. The gates opened.

"Can I come watch television with you later?" he asked.

"Sure," I said.

Lamont still insisted that he had mental problems. Just because he was quiet and didn't bother anyone I thought. He was tall, and wasn't ugly, and I knew if he was to clean himself up he'd be fly.

The gates opened at seven o' clock on the dot. The guy stood outside my cell—I didn't even know his name. I lay in my bed gathering my thoughts: mostly thinking about home and how I couldn't wait to see my family. The anticipation was killing me. I prayed hard for God to help me make it.

When the cell opened, Lamont left and went to David's. The guy slipped in. He put a piece of cardboard over the toilet seat and sat on top of it. I looked at him and asked his name.

"Larry," he said. How common. We had a general conversation about life and what he did to get himself locked up. He then told me that someone in the jail had poured scalding hot water on him during a fight that he and another inmate were having. (So that was how Mike-Mike ended up in the hole.) He showed me the burn marks on his back. They were awful. I knew that must have been painful. He went on talkin' about how pretty my lips were and I was sitting there wishing for him to kiss them.

"Would you like a kiss?" I asked. I didn't see any point in waiting any longer. He just kept talking about them, we might as well put them to use.

"No," he answered.

I felt used. All this time he was in my face wasting my precious time when I could be running around looking for cigarettes for A.J. At least if I would have asked A.J. for a kiss he would have said yes. Then Larry ran out of the cell and never came back. What a loser.

I went upstairs and talked to A.J through the gate. The more I talked to A.J the deeper I fell for him. I loved the way he'd stand in his cell with his boxers on and his dick just hanging. I stared at the print through the bars. He laughed. I laughed. That was my baby.

I was getting more admirers on the block. More and more people would come to my cell telling me how cute I was and how Lamont was ugly. I thought that was really bad for them to say that about my sister. As long as Lamont had a friend like me that was all he needed. I'd always be in his corner, even when the times got rough and he missed home. He didn't have any family to send him money like I did. He would talk to his sister now and then on the phone but that was about it. Lamont and Tracy even stopped speaking because Lamont didn't tell him that just three days ago Bullet had come in my cell and showed me his dick. Apparently Bullet screamed it out one day when he was beating up on Tracy in the cell. That was terrible. From then on Tracy couldn't stand Lamont. But he would talk to me. It seemed like Lamont was the most hated person on the block. He couldn't even get a haircut without a hassle.

A.J. had written me the sweetest letter. It gave me goosebumps. When I couldn't see him up close, I would take my mirror and put it through the bars and watch him. I was kind of sad since I was leaving on Saturday. I wished I had gotten to know him a little better before I left. Although

I did start to feel as though he was taking advantage of me. Every time he needed a cigarette or something to eat, my dumb ass would be right there for him. I was spreading myself very thin trying to please him. But I couldn't stand the thought of being by myself or being on B-block without him. I needed a thug like him in my life. I was glad to have met him. He gave me something to look forward to when the gates opened.

Anthony was my brother away from my brother. He was a rock solid heterosexual and wasn't at all threatened by my homosexuality. He didn't care how gay I was. I'd stand in my cell and dance in front of him and he'd laugh.

"I'm not like that, but if I was you'd be the first one I'd go to," he said.

I had no sexual feelings towards him but what he said sure did put a smile on my face. Tracy was still crazy about him.

Even though I was getting all my props from the people on B-block telling me that I looked good, I still wanted to go home.

Friday came quick. It rained. I stayed in my cell all day. I didn't have any reason to roam the block. I didn't want to see A.J. just yet. I wanted to make him sweat. Everyone was asking me why I wasn't happy to be going home. For some reason the excitement wasn't overcoming me like I thought it would. I called my mom and she was glad I was coming home tomorrow. She said she would be there first thing in the morning to get me.

I finally went upstairs to talk to A.J., after he yelled out my name over a dozen times. He looked pitiful standing there with his nose between the bars. All I could say was that I was leaving tomorrow. All he wanted to know was what I was leaving him. I told him I would be back and I went back to my cell. I looked at my sentencing sheet over and over again praying to God that I would be able to finish my community service after I got out.

I made my rounds on the block before lockdown time. Bullet gave me his home telephone number and address. My heart was beating a thousand times per minute. I was just hours away from being at home, sitting in my living room where I had not been for seven months. Sleeping in my bed...to calm myself I talked to Lamont and sang songs for about two hours before I fell asleep. It seemed like the night was never gonna end. The rain started to fall. I lay in the bed listening to the raindrops hit the windowpane. I slept very comfortably.

I turned over and glanced at the time on the television. It was seven o' clock. I got up from my bed and looked on the top bunk where Lamont was still asleep. I walked over to the window and closed it. The draft from the damp air was beginning to get to me. I had anticipated that the gate would be open. It wasn't. I turned around to lay back in the bed and watch cartoons. Eight o' clock came. The gate was still closed and locked. I was just waiting to hear the loud roar from the gate and the CO calling my name. The gate remained shut. I wrapped myself up tighter under my sheets and continued to stare at the dirty off-white bars. 8:15 a.m. Maybe my mother hadn't gotten there yet. Maybe she was running a little late because of traffic or her car wouldn't start. Eight thirty, all gates opened. It was time for morning let out. I got up, sat on the side of the bed, and turned off the TV. I ran out of the cell to the dayroom to use the phone. I called my mom, no answer. I tried again two hours later, still no answer. I called my grandmother and explained to her that I was supposed to be released today, but she didn't know where my mother was either. I called home again and my mother picked up the phone.

"Hello," she said in a weary voice.

"What happened?" I asked, excitedly.

"I was just there and they said that they didn't have any paperwork on you being discharged today and that I have to call over to records Monday morning." My heart just dropped. I held the phone closely to my ear, just panicked. She told me that she would be up there to see me tomorrow and bring me some money for some underwear. After hanging up the phone I went into my cell where Lamont was sitting on the edge of my bunk watching cartoons. He stood up and opened his arms to hug me. I graced his body with the front of mine, sadly, and then we sat down. I reached under the mattress to get my sentencing sheet and noticed that, in fact, I did need to complete community service before I could be released. I put the paper back in the envelope and pulled out my calendar. The last day on the calendar was marked off, and I was still sitting here. I folded the piece of paper up and placed it back in the envelope. I grabbed my pillow and lay down to watch Saturday morning cartoons with Lamont.

All that day I stayed in my cell. I didn't want people coming to ask me what happened, although they still did. I waited 'til later on in the day before I went to see A.J. He said he knew I wasn't going anywhere. Speaking to him was a drag. I went back to my cell and cried. I couldn't take listening to the radio, I couldn't eat, and I couldn't sleep. All I could do was cry. My underwear was dirty and my t-shirt was sweat stained. I tried washing them by hand but that just wasn't working. Anthony came to my cell to talk to me and comfort me. He told me that everything was gonna be all right and he was there if I needed him.

The next day both my mother and grandmother came to visit. I had to wear dirty, wet underwear out to see my family because I had dropped my underwear in the shower. I was happy to see my mother and my grandmother. My grandmother kept looking around at the other inmates snickering, wondering what they did to get put in here. She was very inquisitive about the place. She had never been to a prison before. I had on my shower shoes and my feet were very cold. She said that that was my punishment. I laughed when all I really wanted to do was cry. I sat at the opposite side of them in the chow hall as we talked about different things. My mother brought me a money order for fifty dollars for food and underwear.

"Thanks," I said. I needed that.

A.J was not speaking to me. Someone asked him if he was my boyfriend and he told them no.

He was starting to put on an act in front of his friends. Another boy from PC tried to confront me, wanting to know why I was putting up with A.J.'s shit. He wanted to be my man. His name was Vernon. Vernon was arrested for raping a little boy so I didn't want any part of him. I showed everyone the letters that A.J. wrote to me to make him look like the fool. He stated that he was only using me to get cigarettes and anything else he needed and wanted. Were my eyes opened! I hated him. I just sat in my cell holding my pillow tight and cried. All of A.J.'s letters were spread out on my bed. I flushed six of them down the toilet and kept the rest for memories.

Shyheed got fired from the trailers and, surprising as it may seem, moved to B-block. I knew I was cool now. His cell was right across from mine. My big brother was now on the same block as me; he wouldn't let anyone fuck with me.

I couldn't believe A.J. played me. I thought he was definitely the one. Vernon wrote me a letter saying that he thought I was attractive but I never responded. A.J. came out of his cell before we had to lock down. He looked good. He didn't say one word to me. He walked down the steps to a table where he started to play chess. When it was time for lock up I went to my cell, grabbed my mirror, and stuck it out of the gate to watch his every move. I sat down on the side of my bed.

Lamont wasn't feeling well. He came down with a bad cold. I needed to be there for him and take care of him like he always did for me. I tried to fluff his pillows, but they just wouldn't fluff. Instead, I told him stories off the top of my head, which he loved.

I felt like I was on the *Young and The Restless.* A.J. wrote me a letter that the CO dropped through the gate. I picked it up and read it, with Lamont hovering over my shoulder.

Wassup Baby Thug?

I know you don't wanna hear from me now, but, I want you to know that I'm very sorry for what I did to you. I love you more than anything in this world right now. You are always there for me when I need you. I don't knowwhat I would do without you. I'm just sitting here thinking about how I never felt this way for another dude. You have something special about you that I like, and when we both get out I'm gonna show you how much I care for you. I noticed that you've been admiring my dick print and I know you wanna see it bad. Well tonight, you're gonna see it. Please don't be mad at me, Baby Thug, okay. Everything's gonna work out fine.

Love Always,

Daddy Thug

My eyes watered up. Lamont was just as surprised as I was.

"So what you gonna do?" asked Lamont. I really didn't have an answer for him just yet.

"Let me think about it," I said.

Anthony read the letter.

"You better take this and run with it," he said.

Me, Anthony, and Lamont walked upstairs to the gate. Anthony acted as if he was the divorce court judge that didn't want to grant the divorce. He played the peacemaker while Lamont stood around and watched. I stood there in my long johns and blue gym shorts looking at A.J. Vernon was at the gate of his cell peeping in. A.J. explained that he wanted to be with me and he was sorry. I smiled. Vernon had a disappointed look on his face, yelling to me that A.J. didn't deserve me. I knew that. I just loved going for a ride with a thug.

Lamont was feeling better. He was well enough to go to chow himself. As we passed center to get to the chow hall Lamont's CO fans were cheering for him, happy he was well. They were yelling out 'Laverne,' their nickname for him. I laughed. They laughed.

Everything was starting to fall into place, but I certainly didn't think things were moving fast enough. I was informed that I would be able to go back down to pre-release on Wednesday to finish up community service. I was tired of trying. I knew I was never gonna see home, but I felt it was my duty not to give up. I had come too far to turn back now.

During my sleep I heard the loud roar of the gate opening at six o' clock in the morning for breakfast. I thought about A.J. the entire night. I just had to see him. I asked the CO who was posted on his block if I could see him. He told me no. But then he was staring at me with a funny look on his face, a half smile. I looked at him questioningly.

"If I do you a favor, you have to do me a favor," he said. I wondered what he was in to.

"What are you talking about?" I asked.

"Suck my dick, and I'll will let you see him," he said. Everyone on B-block was at the chow hall for breakfast, so whatever I decided it would have to be quick.

"Fine," I said. The CO opened the gate. I ran past him and up the steps to A.J.'s cell. I yelled out his name in a deep whisper so I didn't wake anyone else up. He was lying there on the bed, his naked feet poking out. I called him again telling him to wake up. He looked up at me trying to open his eyes. I just smiled at him.

"All right, c'mon," the CO hollered out to me. I ran back down the steps. People were returning from breakfast. The CO unzipped his pants.

"C'mon," he said. "Real quick."

I insisted that we would have to do it later because I didn't want to get caught. He zipped up his pants with a disappointed look on his face. I ran back to my cell and got in the bed. Lamont came in from breakfast and couldn't believe what I had told him. I had seen A.J. I could relax now. I went back to sleep.

Only two more days on the block 'til I moved back to pre-release. I had spoken with the counselor to make sure this was the schedule. I was sick of getting my hopes up for nothing.

Lamont and I were going to dinner later that evening when I turned my head to notice the sexiest boy I had ever seen. I don't usually like dark-skinned guys but he was fine as ever. Barry was his name. He was moving to B-block. I was so excited. I couldn't wait to finish eating and get back to the block. He was tall with wavy hair that looked as if he just had a shape-up done--so cute. He had just turned 18, so he was moving up from the juvenile block. *Sexy Chocolate* was what I called him and I had to have him. He looked at me and I turned my head and blushed. Then he walked pass me and emptied his tray in the trash. Back on the block, I stared at him the whole night. Barry was from Chester so he knew just about everyone, even A.J. He and A.J. would have conversations through the gate and I watched. I didn't want Barry to know that I knew A.J. so I just stayed away when they were conversing. Tracy came on the block to speak to Barry. That was my ticket to get to know Barry a little better. Tracy introduced the two of us. Barry got Tracy to give him two cigarettes. Tracy could see the glare in my eyes and he knew where I was going with it. I needed Barry bad and he was on the same block with me so there was no reason why I couldn't have him.

"He's a freak," Tracy said.

Hmm, I thought. What can I do to get him? The early part of the evening I spent my time writing a letter to Barry.

Wassup Playa?

I been checkin' you since I first laid eyes on you. I think you are sexy as hell and I need you bad. I could just taste your satisfaction in my mouth right now. I would eat you as if you were a Snickers Bar and swallow you like Hot Chocolate. I'll make you cum one thousand times. I know you want it too. But whatever you decide, let's do it fast because I'm leaving the block tomorrow.

Sincerely,

Reg

I was getting hot writing it to him. I could just imagine how he tasted. I couldn't wait. Tracy had already told him I had a crush on him and looked at me and winked. My neck and face instantly flushed. I walked up to him, secretly passed him the note and he whispered in my ear that he'd holla at me lata. I went back into my cell and sat on the side of the bed to watch *Oprah*. Lamont knew that I had a crush on Barry but didn't want to say anything since he and Tracy still weren't talking. I grabbed Lamont's hand, walked him to the door of A-block, and called for Tracy. The three of us stood there by the door. I wanted them to be friends again. I told them that I thought it was stupid to stop being friends because of another man's stupidity. Somehow I got them to agree and they hugged. I was happy to know that after I left the block Lamont would still have a friend to talk to.

The sun was going down. We were locked down because someone in the women's division set fire to the bed and jumped in it trying to commit suicide. Hmm, I never thought of that one. Anyway, the gates opened at six o'clock for dinner. I grabbed my plastic cup and fork and walked with Lamont to the chow hall. They were serving hamburgers. I was extremely hungry and wanted the meal to last so I ate slowly, not realizing the romantic night in store for me. I sipped my juice and watched the COs walk around the tables. I waited for Lamont before I got up to empty my tray. We walked back to the block together. I waited in my cell watching *Martin*. At 7:05 p.m. the gates opened. I didn't want to make it look like I was pressed so I waited until my show went off before I went hunting for Barry. At 7:30 p.m. I walked to the doorway of the cell where I saw him doing push-ups on the bar below the steps. I walked over to him.

"Wassup?" I asked.

He smiled. I smiled.

"I have a girlfriend and besides I don't go that way," he said.

My mouth dropped. All of that for nothing. I didn't even feel like asking any questions. I just turned around and walked back to my cell hoping that he'd follow. He didn't. Lamont came in the cell and asked me what happened. I really didn't want to talk about it. He told me he would be down at David's cell if I needed him. I stared at the TV screen. I wanted to go home.

Anthony came in the cell, he saw me sitting there watching TV alone.

"What's wrong with you?" he asked. I turned around and looked at him. He sat down on the piece of cardboard that was placed over the toilet seat.

"I need some bad," I answered.

He raised his eyebrows and smiled, asking me about Barry. I told him the story and he listened. I told him how much I wanted Barry and how I was so disappointed. Lamont came into the cell and looked at me with a smile. He grabbed his magazine and walked back out. Anthony looked at me, I looked at him.

"Come sit next to me," I said.

He laughed. "Reg, I don't go that way," he said.

"Man, just come sit on the bed," I demanded. He came and sat next to me. He leaned back.

"So wassup?" I asked. I then looked down at his dick. I got up to put the sheet over the bars and sat back down next to him on the bed.

"What you doing?" he asked. "I told you, man, I don't knock ya'll for what yall do but I don't go that way," he continued. I looked at him and placed my hand on his hard dick. He looked at me with an evil look in his eyes and removed my hand.

"So, you don't wanna do nuffin?" I asked.

He let out a big sigh and turned his head.

"Shit, we might as well since you already touched it," he replied.

I pulled down his brown pants to his ankles. I could see his love muscle throbbing through his white boxers. I grabbed it and pulled it out. I could feel his straight pubic hairs touching my skin. I put the head of his dick between my lips and massaged it with my tongue. He licked his lips. I went down on the rest of his dick feeling the tip in the back of my throat, he gasped. He stood up and leaned me on the bed; he climbed on, and before I knew it he was in me, pumping harder and harder in and out. I groaned, his breath slightly touched my ear. He groaned and I lay there. His moans got louder. I grabbed his back and squeezed. I couldn't wait until it was over but I wanted it just as much as he did. I started to reach my peak as he squirted his liquids out all over. He came, letting out the biggest sigh ever. His toes curled and his legs were shaking. He got up and cleaned himself. I sat up and giggled. I walked over to the sink and wiped down. He looked at me and smiled. I was ready for the shower. I took down the sheet and sat on the side on the bed. He sat on back on the cardboard box. Lamont came in. I licked my lips and Lamont started to laugh.

"I'mma see you lata, Reg," Anthony said standing up.

"Ok," I told him. He left out the cell. I fell back on the bed with relief.

The next day I was leaving for pre-release. I was still thinking about my interesting night. Tracy came on the block and I just had to tell him what happened. He was shocked. He wanted to be the one that turned Anthony out. He looked at me with envy and smiled.

"You go boy!" he shouted.

Tracy and Lamont helped me pack my things. I ran upstairs to say farewell to A.J. I just wanted to say bye, but he wanted to hold a conversation. I gave him two cigarettes, turned around and walked back down the steps with him still screaming words and questions for me to answer. I was gonna miss A.J., Anthony, Lamont, Tracy, and Barry. I walked into my cell where I had to get the rest of my things. Tracy and Lamont helped carry my things to the dayroom. Bullet was playing pool. I went over to him and he gave me a hug trying to feel on my butt, but he didn't succeed. He wanted some of me bad. He was mad as hell that he couldn't have me—I could see it in his face. I said goodbye to everyone that was in the dayroom. I gave Tracy and Lamont a hug. Back down the hill.

Back to Pre-release

On my way out I glanced outside at the basketball court so I could get another look at Sexy Chocolate one last time. He knew I was leaving but I guess he didn't want to say goodbye. I didn't like him any more anyway, because he let A.J. read the letter I wrote him. But I wasn't ever gonna see either one of them again, so it didn't matter. I was going to miss Lamont though. The only thing that got on my nerves about him was that he begged too much. He always wanted someone to give him a cigarette or some food. One night he kept me up yelling to the CO for a cigarette. That got on my nerves. I was glad that was over.

I walked down to outtake with Barry and A.J. still on my mind. I thought about what A.J. would do while I was gone. I waited down at outtake in the holding cell for the rest of the fellas. I sat there and thought about how much fun I'd had on B-block. After about a half-hour we all rode the van down to pre-release. It was kind of chilly outside. I sat in the back of the van and looked out of the window while riding down the hill. I glanced over to my right and saw that they were just about finished with the new jail. It was larger than the existing jail and much cleaner. I was glad I wasn't moving in there. I'd heard that no one could smoke in there and that the windows were very tiny and wouldn't be able to be opened.

I walked through the doors. Butler was sitting there, playing cards. He turned to me and smiled, then Mark ran to the door smiling at me. They were happy to have me back. Hell, I was happy to be back. Tyriq had already left to go home. I was happy for him. I was lead to the weekender side where I had to sit through the whole speech about the rules and regulations again. I guess I needed that huh? Sitting there, all I could do was think about A.J. After the speech was over I called my mom to let her know I was back down the hill. James walked past me and went straight to his bunk. I was surprised to see him down here. I pulled on the tail of his shirt. He turned around and looked at me.

"Can you do my hair?" he asked.

"Damn, I can't get a hello?" I said. "Soon as you see me, that's the first thing you got to say?" I continued.

He laughed as he grabbed for a porno book from under his pillow.

Arnold smiled when he saw me.

"Wassup," he said. "Don't take ya' ass over the weekender side no more," he told me in a playful mood. I smiled at him.

"Very funny," I replied. I walked around to get myself familiar with the place again. Mark was getting things ready for dinner. I told James I would braid his hair later, after I had gotten myself settled in. I went to my cube, which was located up in the front where I was before. I shared the front cube with a boy named Robert, who was the same person I had shared a cube with the first time I was down here. I didn't get along with him at all.

Later that night I sat on the top bunk, thanking God for allowing me to make it back down the hill safely. Before I went to sleep I looked around the room and saw nothing but total darkness, except for the lights coming from the guards' office. I lay my head down on the pillow for a good night's rest.

The next day my mother came to visit. Again, she brought me ten dollars worth of quarters. She kept saying it was just a matter of time before I was released. I was almost beyond believing that. I was glad to finally be able to taste vanilla ice cream. I had brought an ice cream sandwich with some of the quarters. The rest were for me to make phone calls at the pay telephone.

I didn't go to community service for about a week. I stayed back for seven days with James. He and I had to cut the grass that surrounded the new prison. I was very cold. I had on my orange-hooded sweatshirt with D.C.P. written on the back and a pair of old Reebok sneakers. The women were already moved over into the new prison. When James and I were cutting the grass they came to the window. I stood out there in the cold. The windows were in a rectangular shape and it was hard for them to see through it. James was getting a kick out of it all. They were flashing their chests and James was flashing his dick. They were telling me how cute I was and that they wanted to see my dick. They also wanted to know how old I was. I didn't want to see them licking on each other's nipples, so I just smiled at them and turned back to cutting grass. I couldn't wait until four o'clock so I could go back inside and rest. My hands were cold and I was hungry. I was missing home bad.

The nights weren't moving fast enough and still no community service. It seemed as if nobody wanted to take me out with them. CO Tony and I didn't get along, and John was out sick. I was depressed. Here it was just a matter of time before I could be released, but I couldn't go anywhere until I did my community service. But nobody would take me out! I needed to see someone about this. Finally my mother called to the prison and got things moving. One good thing, Robert got sent up the hill because he punched a hole in the wall.

The first day of community service was hell. We were chopping down trees that stood on the side of the street. The tips of my fingers were numb. I stood in the middle of the street holding up a yellow sign to the drivers on the road. I never could do manual labor, but the prison sure was making a man out of me.

When I got back up to pre-release, I found out a guy named Terry was now sharing my cube with me. I was very disappointed until he opened his mouth to speak.

"Hey girl," he said in an excited voice, as if he knew me.

I looked at him and all I could do was laugh. He started unpacking his things as he told me his name and what he was in jail for. Terry weighed about 200 pounds and stood at about 5 feet 8 inches. He told me he was bisexual, married and had a child on the way. Hmmm, I thought, another Lamont. Except I could tell he was trying to be in competition with me. He stated he was the queen and I was the princess. He had to complete 200 hours of community service before he could be released, and he was ready for it.

I now had the bottom bunk and Terry had the top. Terry was in his early 30's so he knew all the games the guys here in prison played. We'd lie on our bunks and talk about the different men in the jail we were attracted to.

I wrote A.J. a letter and mailed it back up to the prison hoping that he'd get it before I went home.

Commissary finally came. I bought a pair of long johns and some food. I felt it was only right to share some of my food with Terry. After I finished reading my book, *B-Boy Blues*, I let Terry read it. I sat in my bunk listening to Jay-Z's *It's a Hard Knock Life* on the radio, and bobbed my head to the cute guys that walked past me.

Community service was horrible and so were the two men, Tony and John who headed the group. I got tired of the demands of the prejudiced white people. Chopping and cutting down weeds was all we seemed to do. My legs were hurting from walking up and down the highway picking up trash. My jacket didn't fit and neither did my pants. The crack of my ass was exposed and freezing. Those cold mornings were not good, and neither were the cold afternoons. I wanted to be home at least by Thanksgiving, but it looked like that wasn't going to happen. The boys on the crew turned their noses up at me because I was gay. I'd glance at them, suck my teeth, and turn my head. They would make jokes and Tony would laugh with them. He never allowed me and Terry out together because he thought it was disgusting to see two faggots together. We walked for miles—the crew leaders acting like they were slave drivers. I hated the way they talked to me, like I wasn't human.

The days were slowly passing. We had a job to do right in my hometown. I jumped in the van and we rode to Darby, PA. I was so glad to see it: my school, the barbershop, and the stores. I was right around the corner from my house. We had to clean out the old abandoned building down by the bus depot. I wanted to escape so badly. I was so close to home, yet so far away. I snuck in the office of the building and called my mother on the phone and she was able to bring me some extra money without Tony paying attention. I was so glad I didn't get caught this time.

The next day we raked leaves. The entire football field was covered with leaves. John stood back and watched us rake the whole thing. I was so glad to get back to base. I took a shower and then lay down to read my book. I tried not to fall asleep but couldn't help it. I knew I wasn't gonna get the chance to ever go home. I was working so hard. I talked on the phone everyday to my best friends and my family. I kept hope alive. I knew that God would relieve me someday; I just didn't know when. The community service seemed endless. You can quit school, you can quit your

182

girlfriend, you can quit the basketball team, but you can't quit community service.

Terry started to get on my nerves. He was always trying to outdo me. He thought he looked better than me, and would try to embarrass me by pulling my pants down in front of people. Everyday when I'd call home, my mom would give me words of wisdom. Everything seemed to be pissing me off big time. I was about to snap. This wasn't a good time for my temper to build up because these people weren't worth it. I was tired of the whole scene. I was tired of people harassing me. I couldn't have a general conversation without the word sex coming up. I longed for respect. I longed for dignity.

James only had four days left before he was discharged. Butler was sent back up the hill because he was caught off his post during work hours. James was happy. He was done with community service and in four days he was done with his rehab.

Saturday night I watched videos with Mark and Arnold. Arnold was glad to be leaving in two days. I looked around and noticed that I was going to be here by myself. I had a feeling that's how it was going to happen. I sat there twiddling my thumbs as I watched Faith Evan's video "*Love Like This*." Mark leaned over and whispered in my ear that he wanted me to taste him. I got up and watched him grab for his dick. I left out the cube and went back to mine. I lay in my bed praying silently. Then Terry came in the cube asking me to play cards. I said yes. I needed something to take my mind off things. I couldn't wait 'til Monday morning.

The week was moving slow. We didn't have community service on Tuesday due to Election Day. Then the following Tuesday was Veterans Day. All of a sudden all these damn holidays were popping up out of nowhere.

James' and Arnold's names were called for discharge. James walked quickly to the guards' office. He was happy to be discharged. He gathered his things, and ran out the door and into the van for processing. I stood talking on the payphone when he came back down twenty minutes later because he forgot his certificate for completing the rehabilitation program. At ten o' clock at night, James was finally going home. He came in through the door wearing blue denim jeans with the matching jacket and a pair of sunglasses. I could see the relief on his face when he looked at me and smiled.

"Take care," he said.

I looked at him with envy and smiled. Then he told me Nasir was back in intake. He was caught selling drugs to an undercover cop. I thought about Nasir from H-block and let out a big sigh. I looked up as James walked slowly out the door and hopped in the van with Arnold, who was waiting in the passenger seat. I went back to my bunk to cry. I put my radio up close to my ears and sobbed. The lights went out and I fell asleep.

I wanted to go out on the weekends. John and Tony were taking everyone out on the weekends but me. Tony had a big problem with me and I couldn't stand it. If I was to go out on the weekends that would lessen my hours of community service and I could get home faster.

"No! I am not," Tony growled when I asked him about it.

I was heart broken. I called my mom, and she called his supervisor. The following weekend, I was out for community service. I knew everyone didn't like me, but I didn't care. I was doing what was necessary to get myself out. Tony stood over me watching. Every time I messed up he'd call me a 'fuckin' faggot.' Nothing I hadn't heard before.

Delaware County Prison was in transition. I was lucky not to be going through that shit. Thank you, God.

Since Butler had been moved and James shipped out, I was now left with Terry. Our cubicle was moved towards the back because of newcomers to pre-release. I was happy for that. Terry and I packed our things and moved to our new cubicle. I lay down on my bed and picked up my book to read. I had only two days of community service left. I was so excited.

Our next time out, we were at a warehouse moving large boxes that contained important courthouse information. We had to form a line to pass the boxes. My arms were tired and I dropped a box on my foot.

"Pick up the box, faggot," this white boy said to me. I looked at him.

"Fuck you, bitch," I responded.

He walked over and punched me three times in my face! I was dazed and had a hard time keeping my balance. I staggered over to John.

"He just hit me," I told John, holding my hand over my right eye.

"Get back to working," he said.

I felt like a punk. I then ran over to the white boy and John caught me and slammed me to the ground. I lay there and started to cry. For sure I knew I was not going home now. John lay on top of me until I stopped moving. I stared at the ceiling and gave up.

On the ride back to base my body started to shake. While riding I was looking out of the window watching the trees and the day-to-day life of the streets. When we got back to base the Lord was smiling down on me. John said that he wasn't gonna ship either of us out. Instead he told me that he wouldn't be putting my paperwork through for three more days. I was so happy. I'd rather do three days instead of thirty.

I told my mother what happened and she was furious. The three days went by so slow. I couldn't eat nor sleep. I just talked on the phone the entire time.

The last day of community service and I was happy as hell. No more sucking up to the white man. No more raking leaves, passing boxes, weed plowing, or walking miles and miles a day. I had two more days to go before I could be released.

The next day I went up to the old jail to help clean it. I walked through H-block, B-block, E-block, and F-block. It was kind of nice. I sat down on my old bunks and thought of the times I had shared with people who cared about me. I marked my name on E-block's steps. Love always, Reg... 1998.

I jumped in the van and rode back down the hill. It was getting cold outside and I wanted to get back indoors before I caught a cold. I went inside and took a shower. Terry was upset because he said he was gonna miss me. I told him I'd miss him too. I gave him a hug and left him with all my cosmetics, since I didn't need them anymore. I jumped in bed early, as if I was a child on Christmas Eve. I said my prayers and hurried fast to sleep.

In the middle of the night stomach pains awakened me. I jumped up and hurried myself to the bathroom. After covering the toilet with tissue paper I sat there for about five minutes with nothing happening. I walked anxiously back to my bunk and woke up Terry. He looked at me half asleep and said it was butterflies in my stomach. Well for it to be butterflies, it sure did hurt like hell. I went to the guards' office and the CO gave me a hot cup of tea with lemon but no sugar. It was nasty without the sugar but it worked. I sipped it until it was gone. I rested my head back on my pillow and with the cold November air blowing through my fan I went to sleep.

The morning came. I was happy to be going home. I awakened with a smile on my face. I went to the front door to check on the weather, it was breezy outside. Everyone was on the way out for community service. I stayed back. Lieutenant Blisseron was on duty. I was glad her pretty face would be one of the last faces I would see. I went into the bathroom and brushed my teeth. I ran to the telephone booth to call my mom. There was no answer. I didn't panic. I went back to my bunk to lie down. I watched television. People were passing my cube telling me that I wasn't goin' anywhere. I watched television until I fell asleep. Around one o' clock I woke up and ran to the guards' office for an explanation as to why I wasn't discharged yet.

"Reginald, if I knew anything I would tell you, sweetie. They haven't called yet," she said in a soft voice. Then I ran to the phone to call my mother. Still no answer. I called my grandmom and couldn't find anything out. I called my mother's work number and they said she hadn't been in all that day. I walked slowly back to my bunk and sat on the bed. My eyes started to water. The tears fell from my eyes like a raging waterfall. I couldn't stop crying. I nervously wiped my eyes, stood up, and walked back to the guards' office.

"They didn't call yet?" I asked very loudly.

"No Reginald they hav…" but the ringing phone cut her off. She picked it up and I continued to stand there. She turned around to me, her eyes full of tears.

"Goodbye Reginald," she said smiling. I grinned from ear to ear, like a faggot in boys' town.

Outtake

I waited out there in the cold for about thirty minutes before they decided to open the gates. I had to go up to the new prison's outtake. I walked in and looked around. It seemed like a maximum-security prison. I didn't say anything to nobody. I kept my mouth shut. I had all of my belongings in a blue net bag in my left hand, and my television in my right. I went into a holding cell where I changed out of my browns into my street clothes that were too big. Looking at the people that were coming in off the street, I just shook my head. They were laughing at me in my too-big clothes, not realizing that I was laughing at them. They didn't know how hard their road was going to be. After changing my clothes, I signed a few papers and was out the door. The gusty wind hit my face as soon as I walked outside. I jumped in the front seat of the van and we drove to the top of the hill where I saw the top of my mother's car. And there she was in the driver's seat. The CO stopped the van and smiled at me.

"Good luck," he said. I shook his hand and hopped out of the van. I walked over to my mom's car as she popped the trunk and I put my things in. I got in the passenger side of the vehicle and we drove away into the glorious sunlight.

-Delaware County Prison-